DJUMBOLA

DJUMBOLA

Gavin Murtagh

ATHENA PRESS
LONDON

DJUMBOLA
Copyright © Gavin Murtagh 2005

All Rights Reserved

No part of this book may be reproduced in any form
by photocopying or by any electronic or mechanical means,
including information storage and retrieval systems,
without permission in writing from both the copyright
owner and the publisher of this book.

ISBN 1 84401 387 1

First Published 2005 by
ATHENA PRESS
Queen's House, 2 Holly Road
Twickenham TW1 4EG
United Kingdom

Printed for Athena Press

*To Frances, Iain, Sarah and David.
Thank you for keeping me focussed on what had to be.*

Also a big thank you to all at Athena for believing in my work.

Foreword

It has always been so. The slaying of a High Priest within Nature is forbidden. Since this slaughter took place a very, very long time ago we have sent ambassadors amongst you only for each to receive a similar fate. Until you rid yourselves of our executioners, mankind's fate is sealed. We come to you one more time. This is your last chance. There will be no other. Our patience is exhausted.

SAHARIAH-ARUN-ALTU

Highest Priestess. Holder of the key. Silent Witness to all. She blessed be.

In the beginning the magic was pure. Harmonious, unaffected. Constantly in balance with nature. ***They*** *came forth, demanding the secrets which held together the fabric of* ***all***. *We refused. Always will refuse to reveal that which has meaning for* ***all*** *in existence. Blessed be to those who follow and protect* ***the*** *line.* ***They*** *have since infested mankind and contrived in your world to present a God of Nature to you. This is not so. What God would allow inventions to fly through the air and speed along the earth, disturbing the fine balance of natural harmony? The slow painful erosion of nature through human neglect. No, the God you worship and pray to is one of self-interest, more in keeping with a Mad Scientist. Nature's laws would never allow such self-indulgence. You have been warned!*

DJUMBOLA-ARUN-ALTU

High Priest of all. Nature's own son. Protector of the key. O Wise One, forever blessed be.

Djumbola heard the sizzling of his skin fat as the fire took hold. Felt it... smelt it. His interrogators, having elicited nothing from him, had embarked on this last resort. Unusual, in their experience. Usually they had the sound of a canary singing by this stage. But Djumbola, in his many lives on this earth, had endured. It was always a spectacle. To put fear into anyone who dared to challenge their line. He had either witnessed or been subject himself to crucifixions, beheadings, burnings at the stake, and hangings, including the cutting open and the scattering of innards and limbs – drawn and quartered.

But this time it was different for him. As he languished in his cell awaiting his latest fate, there came a sign. He had been weeping at the futility of yet another life ending at their will. Nothing on the face of it gained, but he was wrong. For the visitation of a spectre gave hope at last. He knew it was time! Every sense within him screamed that the balance was achieved. So much suffering, so many lives. So many dearer ones subjected to their terrible will. After all this time a way back.

Djumbola. The Highest Priest of *all*. Slaughtered that long time ago by those who chose such methods of persuasion as the stretching (rack) and crucifixion (bloodletting), amongst other similar vile practices designed to elicit secrets from tormented souls. As he had neared death, Djumbola had, to himself, cursed his malevolent visitors, but in his final seconds of life he uttered words he later had regretted. This allowed for a partial entry into *all* but without safeguards.

In hindsight, maybe he did it on purpose. He often had wondered, as they made one mistake after another, that they might finally fall back within his grasp. The blind leading the blind, straight back into his unwelcoming arms! Nature was truly wonderful! It had its own agenda – survival! Djumbola had long understood this. Had often cried, '*Enough*! I cannot protect you anymore.' Nature's response was to send the magic, a visitation always leaving Djumbola humbled. A trust unbroken. A line intact.

This occasion was to be so different. Djumbola was accepting his usual fate but suddenly his senses were back with him, as in his cell earlier. He had the urge to face those lackeys given the job now to despatch him to the flames, having failed in their original brief, to elicit those secrets.

Djumbola looked deeply into his executioners' eyes. Gradually the leering expressions changed to looks of concern, and from concern to mild panic. Regarding each other, eyes widening in terror, the masters of the fire were now becoming a lot less comfortable about their task. No, far from comfortable. That natural confidence of the controller over the controlled was now oozing from their systems. They clutched at their bodies, screaming as agony consumed their senses.

The magic had passed through Djumbola, transferring his suffering to his captors – his outer to their inner – allowing them to share his final moments, in the most personal of terms! This was to happen again, through many ages. Djumbola was, if with nothing else, consistent in this regard.

Sahariah watched over him as any woman in her position would, he being the love of her life. She often wept, turning away from atrocity after atrocity.

His captors' superiors would from this point on be aware of Djumbola's potential. Smoking bodies bore witness as an absolute, clear message.

Not that this message would be shared amongst their subordinates. That might deter them from their work. No, the functioning of their inquisitional expertise must not be in any way affected by something as minor as having knowledge that the suspect might have kinetic powers!

Additionally, the line of impure blood relied implicitly on their seers throughout the ages. Picking up on the prophecies and predictions of each birth of those who would challenge their bloodline and expose them for the upstart race they were. These psychics were now after this latest event, under increased pressure to deliver this information as accurately as possible.

Djumbola had long learned the art of casting false trails, always entering on a blind side. Each life was a learning of more subtle ways in which to make the final incision. He even joined esoteric societies, reaching high status and thus learning so many of their secret ways. To remain one step ahead, Djumbola took much care.

His senses were honed – as sharp as a sultan's scimitar... and in any battle of wits, just as deadly!

Chapter One

Calvin Tulley was a dreamer. He dreamed of many things. Finding a mother lode was a much hoped for experience. He cut a lonely figure out there on the tundra, with only reptiles and insects as company. Slowly he moved along the ground, sweeping his metal detector from left to right and back again, in a world of his own. Hour after painstaking hour he spent, attempting to follow strict lines, so he did not miss much ground. The most Cal had found in his many months of searching was a small hoard of coins. Excited initially, he was soon to discover that most old coins were not very scarce. But it did not dampen his enthusiasm. And it required a hell of a lot of patience to be out there in all weathers with such a slim chance of finding anything worthwhile.

Feeling just a little tired, and with dejection settling in, he sat on a boulder, which made a surprisingly comfortable seat. Opening his flask of hot coffee he scanned the terrain, choosing which direction to go in. As if it made much difference, he thought. He wondered what Sara, the girl from the office, was doing right now. Cal really had a soft spot for her, and wondered if she might like to accompany him on one of these outings. But he considered this too risky to ask her. Cal was not the type to take rejection lightly. He would ponder it, though. In the meantime it would still be subject of his daydreaming!

Refreshed after his drink, which had warmed his innards and helped to cast off the dejection, he was ready to continue. Cal rose and stretched. Looking at the sun's position he could tell there was not much light left. So he decided to walk a tight arc back towards his vehicle – some two miles, he reckoned. But judging time and distance were unfortunately not Cal's best attributes. So often he had drifted way too far before turning back. Then he'd find himself stumbling and falling in the darkness, always bruised and bloodied by the time he got back. This time was to be no exception. But the circumstances were to be entirely unique!

Cal quickened his pace. Suddenly the detector began to vibrate. At the same time his earphones were picking up the sounds of drumming: native drums. Cal looked around him, expectantly. Where are those drums? Nothing in sight. Just sound emitting from the phones. Then the drumming had background: birds singing, other creatures screeching, as in a jungle backdrop. Cal was no expert, but he was thinking the drumming was African, maybe. And with the sounds in the total mix it could be a tropical scene somewhere. But he was here alone in the desert. Well, so Cal thought. Cal was beginning to feel a degree of excitement. That – and also a little fear mixed in. But, he thought, this whole deal is totally phenomenal!

He stopped at the point where he thought the object was hidden. The drumming was now so loud he removed his headphones, laying them down on the ground. But he could still hear the drums and other commotion clearly without them! Again he looked around him. For the noise to be this loud they should be in sight... but nothing. He considered, Am I going crazy? The detector began to shake, bringing Cal back to the job in hand. It was shaking so much he had difficulty holding on to it. Suddenly, it shot from his grasp, into the ground. The bottom edge disappeared, lodged solid. Cal got on his hands and knees. First he tried to pull the metal detector out of the ground. Nothing doing. It was jammed fast! Then he started to dig around it with the small sharp fork he used for excavation, being careful not to disturb the contents of the ground too much in case the object was fragile. Cal had been on a dig. He knew the importance of subtle digging.

Cal found the head of the detector had attached itself to a small rock about the same size as a tennis ball. Again, he tried to dislodge the detector from the rock but it still stuck hard. 'Magnetic?' Cal whispered to himself. 'Some force pull, if so.' Christ, it was getting dark too. As he picked up the two fastened objects he placed the rock into the palm of one hand and held the end of the stick in the other. The rock appeared to be some kind of quartz. It felt warm to the touch and began to vibrate ever so gently. Cal peered closely at it. Being short-sighted, and not risking his glasses on any of these trips, he was not able to define the many particles within it. He had also not as yet realised that the setting around him had changed, being so wrapped up in studying the rock. His failing eyesight did not help either. For now the scene had changed to a jungle backdrop, and the drummers could now be clearly seen. Well, clearly in most others' eyes – but not for poor Cal! He could just about make out that each drummer was dressed in some form of cloak with hood drawn up over the head. Cal began to perspire with the new form of heavy heat surrounding him. Sweat began dripping off his nose.

Cal laid the objects down on the ground, jumping to one side at the same time as a creature he could not identify crawled close by him. He felt totally bewildered. The rock began to glow ever brighter as the drumming became faster. Then all of a sudden it rose from the ground, having disengaged from the metal detector. The rock hovered in front of Cal. Then the backdrop began to fade. He found himself back in the desert. The rock back in his hand re-engaged with the detector. Cal was now more confused than ever. What strange tricks were being played on him, and why?

Another thing dawned on him. Not only had the scene changed back but the drums had also ceased. He couldn't recall when they had stopped. Maybe when the rock had landed back in his hand. He just could not remember. The rock was still vibrating. 'Why are you shaking, little one? Are you afraid? No need to be scared of me. Calvin will take good care of you,' he heard himself say. Cal thought if anyone witnessed him talking to a rock he was sure to be sent to the nearest funny farm – somewhere he thought most people believed he had escaped from!

Then he went down, having tripped on an old root. First blood of the day! Slight head wound. Nothing much. The rock had unfortunately flown from his hand as he fell. He was now on his hands and knees patting the ground, but could not locate it. He stood up, swaying slightly. Slight concussion, maybe, he thought. He was feeling very woozy. As best he could he held the detector out in a sweep around him. Nothing. What now?

'Damn, and here was I telling it that it was safe with me! *I* am not even safe with me!' He began to stagger back towards his Jeep, not realising he was headed in the exact opposite direction. Then, out from nowhere, a bright light circled him. It dipped down and back into the palm of his hand. The rock vibrated and began to glow brighter. Cal saw this but couldn't believe it. I am going to wake up with some sore head after this dream, he thought. He looked down at the illuminated piece of space rock. 'Sorry, little fella. Hope I didn't hurt you too much with the fall.'

Cal was considering that he should be afraid. But what the hell, he thought. A rock from the ground appeared to be more friendly to him in a matter of minutes than some human beings could manage in a lifetime. Anyway, what was going on? The rock had found him. It was like, well, it was *alive*! What happened back in that jungle scene? he thought. Was that all for real?

Cal had no more mishaps on the rest of the journey back to his parked vehicle. The light from the rock ensured this, having first turned him around and then borne most of his shifting weight as he swayed and lumbered along. The rock had really taken to Cal, shining a torchlight in front, holding him up, leading him in the right direction. Perhaps even saving his life. For if he had continued in that opposite direction, who knows where he would have ended up – especially in his concussed state.

Cal was again feeling very woozy by the time he reached the comparative safety of his vehicle. 'I know,' Cal muttered confusedly to himself as he got into the Jeep, 'I am still out cold. I went down and bumped my head worse than I thought. As this is all imagination through concussion, it can't be for real. Better not drive. I will just wait here. Perhaps sleep a bit. See how I am first thing in the morning.'

He wrapped himself in a blanket, lay down on the rear seat, and eventually went off. He had many weird dreams that night, some remembered, others not.

Cal woke with a thumping headache. Not so much the after effects of the fall but the crouched position he had slept in. As he opened one bleary eye, discovering the half-light of dawn, he found himself peering out of his covers at a little rock. It was sitting on the seat beside him, inches from his face, vibrating gently.

Calvin Tulley was a single man of twenty-six years. Considered a geek by many, with his horn-rimmed glasses and short-sightedness. A few centimetres short of six feet tall, he was robust in body. In fact, it wasn't a bad frame at all. Just, he considered, it did not make for a good match with his head and feet!

Living alone, Cal often missed mealtimes, engrossed in his surfing of the Internet. The only times he ate regularly were during, and especially after, one of his treks; also on other occasions to clear the fug caused by too much screen watching.

On arriving home, despite still feeling a little fragile, Calvin was ravenous. No ordinary hunger for him. It would be mountains of food before collapsing into a heap in front of the computer. The tiny rock sat on the kitchen table watching Cal's take on a John Candy eating contest. Cal tried to ignore it, turning his back on the rock. He was about to take another mouthful of his fifth bowl of Crunchy Surprise when he found the rock hovering in front of his nose. Cal turned his back again, only for the rock to follow suit! Back in front of his nose. This happened a couple of times more before Cal gave up, putting the bowl down on the table. He was pretty miffed and walked out into the room which housed his extremely high-tech computer system. His brother had set it up for him, being the real expert. He'd given Cal a lot of tips, and spent hours with him before that dreadful day. Cal didn't like to think too much about it. Hurting still, he missed his brother like mad.

The rock was now beside him again. Cal went to switch on the system but it appeared to be already functioning. When he touched the keyboard it was red hot. He let out a yelp and fell back off his chair onto the floor.

The screen lit up. A message appeared seemingly from this little friend. <Overeating is not good for you, Calvin. It is just an observation. And your brother is fine.>

Cal blinked his surprise as he got up and sat down in front of the computer again. He looked down at the rock. 'You can do that? Speak to me through the system? And my brother – how did you know about him?'

More was added to the message on the screen. <So many

questions, Calvin! But that is to be expected. A lot has been going on around you. E was part of that. He came home. Think of it as that. He is fine. You dream of him, I know. He will come to you again. I am told there will be asked of you some things to do. But enough now. Tomorrow will be an enlightening day for you. Go and rest.>

Cal sat for a few minutes reflecting on all of the happenings over the past few hours. His head was spinning now, not just with the after-effects of concussion but also with this whole new situation presenting itself to him, leaving him dazed and not just a little confused. How did the rock know my bro – even the shortened version as a nickname? 'E' for Iain... Got to go and lie down. Seems I will need to be fresh tomorrow to take in more of this whole business.

As he rose from the chair, Cal stumbled. He was going down again until the rock got under him and righted the situation. Cal was still so full of his own thoughts he didn't realise the rock had saved him, again!

Cal's sleep that night was fitful. Again the dreams. He woke up a couple of times, lifting himself up from his prone bedtime position to make sure the rock was still in view. Which it was, still sitting by the computer. It was emitting a slight glow, and a very slight vibration against the desktop caused a barely audible humming sound. It was soothing rather than annoying. After the second wakening, Cal slipped back down into the covers, feeling reassured everything was fine. Then, in a deep sleep, he dreamed of a conversation with E.

Chapter Two

Cal set off the next day with a renewed sense of purpose. He couldn't quite believe it himself. He felt different in a way hard to explain even if he had had to do so. Cal sensed an assertiveness in himself which previously was definitely unknown to his being. He hoped he could keep it up for that day, at least! He need not have concerned himself on that score. Throughout the whole day his work standard was amazing. Insurance underwriting was not ever going to set any fantastic records in business profiteering, but nevertheless it was, to Cal, an important enough position. And his bosses could not fail to be impressed with this day's effort. No little part was played, though, by the small vibrating bulge in his trouser pocket!

Most impressed of all was a little lady sat on the opposite side of the office. She was looking curiously out of the corner of her eye at the day's events in Cal's corner. She decided to make a five-minute job last an hour and five! All the other office staff were packing up for the day. Soon it was just Cal and Sara Alonso left in the room.

Sara was more than aware of Cal's feelings towards her. But up until now she had not wished to give any confusing signals to him, any real sign of returned affection; especially given her poor track record up until now with boyfriends. She had decided on not particularly liking men, but also was aware that at twenty-four years of age she would have to sometime find *the* one to father her babies. 'Romantic' was not Sara's second name! If this was not enough, on top of it there was her temperament. Sara had a wildfire nature. However, being part Nicaraguan, Mexican and Cuban gave some reasoning behind her volatility. Sara was proud of her roots and the peoples she originated from. She was vivacious, and slim in body – and even for her five feet four inches she could pack one hell of a punch. She had been taught by her family at a very young age to defend herself. More than one of her previous boyfriends could give witness to that fact!

Cal looked over at Sara, who was not giving him any return. He had tried to hide that soft spot for her. She was kind and did not make him feel quite the dork he considered himself to be. His computer screen lit up a message. <Go over and talk to her.> Simple and precise.

Cal still could not get his head around the fact that a stone, quartz or whatever, could communicate with him. Especially on such personal lines. But he listened nonetheless and walked over to where Sara was sitting. She looked up at him as he approached and smiled. Cal felt the goosebumps crawling up his arms. He really never knew what to do next, so he just returned the smile which took on more of a grimace.

<You are faltering again, Calvin.> The words appeared on Sara's screen as she looked up at him. He noticed the message, but she didn't, as it disappeared in a flash.

'Don't you ever let up?' Cal hissed quietly.

Sara was frowning now. 'What do you mean? I am just finishing this assignment then I am gone. Do you have a problem with that?'

Cal came to an abrupt stop. 'No – I'm sorry. I wasn't speaking to you. I was speaking to, er, myself.'

Sara was blinking at him, disbelieving. 'Okay you've had one hell of a successful day. No one in this office can be unaware of that. But this woman is not going to bow down and lick your boots because of it like your manager did today.'

'He didn't lick my boots!' Cal now was beside himself. 'Where do you get that from?'

Sara's retort was quick and incisive. 'Maybe he licked somewhere else instead! You disappeared for quite some time with him this afternoon.'

Cal stepped back a pace or two, but instead of feeling the insult he was thinking to himself that she had been watching. Why? Maybe I am in with a slight chance... He was back into dreaming of it when Sara's next retort brought him back to his senses.

'Anyway, what *is* that in your pocket? I know being a woman I am supposed to say that eternal line—' She stopped and waited

18

for Cal's reaction. There wasn't one. 'Well, are you pleased to meet me?' she asked, smirking. Cal just looked questioningly at her. 'Christ, you don't get out enough, Cal!'

Cal stood still for a moment during which another message appeared on her screen. <Time to reveal myself. Are you going to do the honours, or am I?>

Before Cal could react, his trouser pocket felt lighter. The rock was now in the air in front of Sara. She froze, her eyes like saucers. She gulped, then glared at Cal. Before she could speak, another phenomenon was taking place on Sara's computer. This time she did notice it.

<Sara. Hello. This is Calvin. But you already know that. What you do not know yet is that he will make someone – no, not just someone; perhaps that someone is just one. How about it being you? – very happy and contented.>

Sara sat looking at the words on her screen. Shaking her head, she turned to Cal. 'What is going on here? How do you keep that rock in the air at the same time as sending me a message? And what is this all about? Since when have you become a dating agency?'

Cal stood still. 'I am not a magician, Sara. Neither am I interested in forming a dating agency. And I wouldn't use it if I did. Simply, I found me this rock on the last weekend. You know, that metal detecting thing?'

Sara was still glaring. 'And...?'

'And... well, it was a little odd. I fell down after I found it. But then it found me. Helped me back to the Jeep, and communicated with me through the system like it's doing with you.'

The screen illuminated more brightly, a further message imprinted. <Calvin. You have missed out one important fact. Sara is in need of a reliable male for reproductive purposes. Sara, are you not adverse to Cal fathering your babies?>

Cal was about to say something but was shushed by Sara. Something was happening on the opposite side of the office. A slight glow was becoming brighter. Cal's rock left them and proceeded over to that part of the room. At the same time the computer screen was a mass of indistinguishable figures and letters. These began to rotate, slowly at first, then increasing in speed, until finally suddenly coming to an abrupt stop. The rock returned to the pair, and was now sitting on the desk beside Sara's computer.

Sara was not expecting this and shot out of her seat, knocking the desk at the same time. The rock rolled gently towards the floor but Cal instinctively shot out a hand, catching it before it descended. He was amazed at his dexterity. But then he remembered that his little friend could fly! Before he could utter his observations, Cal and also Sara were given a further screen lesson.

<I am just the forerunner for what will be an experience for you both. Please be assured, there is no trickery intended to bamboozle you both. I am as I am. As you are. What will follow me will test you both to the limit. You will succeed. Because you want to succeed. My time with you will be short. I must now bow to those with greater wisdom. Please listen carefully to them.>

The screen went blank. Sara and Cal looked at each other. Cal was about to say something but Sara was getting out of her chair, about to leave. She started to speak to Cal but he hushed her, fingers to his lips and pointing to the other side of the office.

The bright yellow light on the other side of the room was now approaching. From it came the glowing shape of a cloaked and hooded figure, all of six foot plus. It stood before the pair. Both Cal and Sara began to shake. Somewhere from her insides, Sara found words.

'Who are you? And what do you want?'

The figure stood before them completely still. Not a movement for several minutes. Then suddenly it rose further from the ground. Just a matter of inches, but it seemed like a giant forming for the pair of them. Instinctively, Cal held up the rock before the figure. The whole room illuminated a bright green and yellow. The rock vibrated strongly sending tingling sensations down Cal's arm.

'You, Calvin. Yes – you, Calvin. You have held it up to us. You have completed a task we have waited many lifetimes for. Thank you. Do you realise how long we have waited for this time? No! No one in this world could ever imagine. Some things I am permitted to tell you; other facts I am not. Calvin, do you remember the drumming, the figures in the jungle?'

Cal nodded.

'It was our wish that you found the rock for us to energise it in the way you witnessed. We wish to thank you for your part in this process. All is going to plan.'

'What the fuck have you brought us into, Cal?' Sara began to bristle. Cal winced at her tone of voice, never having heard her swear before.

The cloaked figure turned toward Sara. 'Profanity is not in keeping with your true self, Sara.'

'What do you mean? So it's my fault, then? A little bit of swearing from a lady can produce what?' She looked away as the figure came a little closer.

'You have more intelligence than you probably can appreciate. That is being squeezed into too tight a circle. Which is why you feel abject animosity at anything you consider to be a threat to your innerself. Am I correct?'

Sara snorted. 'Analysts get up my nose! And this just sounds like another session.' Cal made as if to hold her hand but Sara took hers away.

'Swearing is a negative. Especially from one who can articulate words in place of it. Intelligence swears in frustration. Others because they know no better. But I have not come here to be your analyst, Sara. And I have little time left now. So please listen closely. There is one here on your earth amongst you, who you will be meeting soon. Fearless... too brave for his own good. But again, who are we to condemn his actions? Could any of us have survived just one of his existences, let alone the many lives he has led until now? What he has achieved in that time is in itself a unique feat. But unique he is and will forever be. He has both helped and hindered us along the way. But that is his way, and we love him all the same.'

The cloaked stranger's head tilted upwards as he spoke. In the front space where normally a face would be expected, instead contained what appeared to be a goldfish bowl! There was a constant changing of images. It seemed like every creature in creation swam in the invisible waters. Both Cal and Sara took steps back.

'Do not be afraid, please. As the rock performs in its form I do so in mine. Do you understand?' Cal nodded agreement. Sara just stared at her feet. 'Good. For I have now very little time. You will be wondering on whom I have been talking about. Calvin, you are keeping up with my rhetoric?'

Cal was not expecting this question. 'I–I mean we – Sara and me... we think we are following this.' He looked at Sara but received a blank.

'You speak for yourself, buster! And you in the hood, why should we be listening to this anyway? We are just little people. Shouldn't you be going to the government? The top people, who always deal with this?'

Cal shifted from one leg to the other, feeling extremely uncomfortable. 'Who is the guy you are talking about? Why can't he approach the top people, as Sara is saying?' he asked the stranger.

'Ah, Calvin. I was told you would be the main one to pick up on these points. Our little friend there has given you some insight, has it not?'

'You mean the rock? Was it really communicating? Don't need to ask that anymore now, huh?' Cal looked over at Sara, who now seemed about to explode. 'But it also said that we – Sara and me – should be a couple and make babies.'

'Yes. Is there a problem with that?' The figure rose another inch or so, but Sara intervened.

'This is not funny any more, Cal. Is this all a ruse? Have you hired this specialist dating agency with all the props just for the benefit of trying to get inside my knickers?' She was not looking at all happy!

Cal was about to reply but the hooded figure spoke. 'You both have to sit down and discuss this matter. For now though please hear me out. There's little or no time left. A very long time ago this world was in constant balance. But those who chose another path through greed and selfishness caused the balance to be disturbed. This created another species of human being. The identification of the source of this particular genus I am not permitted to divulge. Suffice to say it has evolved into the heartless, cruel, sadistic species which has plagued your kind for centuries. However, their grip on this world is tenuous. We have attempted to right the situation, but each time in the past our line ventured forth to attempt a counterbalance, we were increasingly overwhelmed. Your history shows times when certain individuals met their deaths in dubious circumstances. Now you will appreciate another version. Quite simply, you reside in a world whose secrets were stolen from the true line. The big rock was broken and scattered amongst the stars. This has now reformed and is heading back towards your earth. You may call this an asteroid. But to us it is the *Djumbolastone* – so named after our revered and long missed High Priest. Be not mistaken, this stone has but one purpose: to balance the wrongs already inflicted; to destroy or capture this false world's inhabitants and revert *all* back to the true state nature intended for us. We are aware of schemes to deal with this so-called nuisance for the rich people of this planet – to destroy or deflect it from its path. They know not what is being dealt them. Everything they do will be in vain.'

Sara piped up now, clearly interested. She had been listening more intently as the figure went on. 'But surely, some of us do not deserve to go down with those bastards? Surely there is something the rest of us can do?'

'Sara, I am pleased you have understood the points I have attempted to pass on. Of course, there are those we would rather be able to save. But without certain essential tasks being met, we are unfortunately unable to guarantee any kind of success.'

'What kind of tasks?' Cal asked.

'For instance, your little friend there needs to be returned to where you found it. This has completed its own task and would be most grateful for you to return the favour. However, we would not consider it in any way an insult if either of you were to refuse to assist us.'

As these words were spoken the rock rose from its self-induced obscurity to hover in front of the pair.

Cal, for all the feelings he had for his new-found friend, was not about to commit himself. He still felt unsure. His deeply rooted inferiority complex was in play. Sara, on the other hand, appeared to be rejuvenated.

'Of course we will! Come on Cal, these are good enough reasons. All my life I have felt something was not right; far from right. I have always felt that someone has been covering up something – but not as big as this. It's scary. But I am more scared of anything they could do to us than what is hovering in front of me.'

As she spoke, the rock came closer finally resting in the palm of her right hand. Sara didn't now appear to mind! The rock shone a bright luminescence which lit up the room. Cal was speechless, feeling more than a little confused. He also had pangs of jealousy: no longer *his* rock.

The figure spoke. 'Thank you for your kind words, Sara. You are truly meeting with and understanding more than any of our expectations.'

Sara, suddenly not impressed, hissed back, 'You may have a goldfish bowl on your fucking head, but it might as well be a piss pot! You are talking like a man does about a woman all the time in this place – this fucking world! I thought you were supposed to be from another planet. But is it the same for women there as it is here?'

The figure was now retreating. 'I hear your words, Sara, and I am sorry; I would really wish to continue this conversation with you but unfortunately it will have to be on another occasion. The rock will help you in what is required for your first task.'

If it was at all possible, the rock even took on a bright red expression. A light emitting from it appeared to suggest this fact. The figure continued. 'I sense they are on their way, so I must be very quick. Please believe in yourselves. You will always be protected. Stay in the line of truth. The rock will shed shards to you. Keep them. Wear them about your person. I must go now… nearly here…' The voice became fainter and the light disappeared. So did the cloaked figure.

Chapter Three

The office still had partial lighting, allowing the pair to regard each other, waiting for one of them to make the next move. Instead, advice came from the little rock, which was now hovering in front of them. The computer screen lit up with a message.

<Calvin and Sara. It would be to your extreme advantage not to be here in precisely three minutes. Bad people are on their way. I would advise the emergency stairway exit as the best means of escape. Please hurry, my friends.>

Sara was already grabbing up her belongings from the desk. Cal rushed over to the other side of the room, also collecting his briefcase, which by good fortune he had already packed earlier; maybe on the rock's advice, but he could not recall this. A bright light now hovered over the door to the stairway exit, emitting from the rock. Cal grabbed Sara's free hand and both bolted towards the illumination. But Sara stumbled, spilling her bag to the floor.

'Sara, you will have to leave it – we haven't enough time.' Cal was getting frantic.

Sara let go of his hand. 'You go if you want, but this lady never, *never*, goes anywhere without her handbag!'

'So sorry, Sara.' Cal wished he hadn't said anything. Better to have just stooped down and assisted the retrieval of her bits and pieces, which he ended up doing anyway.

<Forty-five seconds> flashed up on the screen nearest to them.

'How does it know all this?' Sarah asked.

'Not the time to ask. Let's *go*!' Cal opened the emergency exit door and both fled down the stairway. Reaching the bottom of the building, Cal opened the door to the street a fraction. As he did so he heard the sound of squealing tyres. A large vehicle came into view, arcing rather than turning round the street corner. The driver appeared to nearly lose it, but corrected with a fierce tug on the steering wheel, causing the whole vehicle to shake. It came to a halt outside the main doors. Four men alighted and rushed the doors. One carried what appeared to be a sledgehammer. The doors were duly trashed and entry gained. *But the doors were already unlocked*, Cal thought to himself. This lot are complete nutters! All they needed to do was just push and walk in. But there again maybe that was their training, like in all the films where the doors are broken down before entry. Or maybe they all had computer chips instead of brains, and could only react in the same way to any given situation. Cal shook his head to stop his thoughts becoming any more bizarre!

With the occupants of the car now inside the building, Cal opened the door a little more, searching the street for the next move. 'Subway,' Calvin thought out loud. 'Pedestrian subway to the other side of the river. Rarely used.'

Sara was now aware of some activity outside, and on hearing the advice began to push open the door, which Cal was still firmly holding on to.

'No, not yet, Sara.'

Sara bristled. 'Why the fuck not? I'm getting very agitated, and that is not good, Cal. Not just for you but anybody.'

Cal was about to reply when another vehicle appeared rounding the corner. He pulled the door back tight and then released it slightly in order to look through the crack at the new arrivals. Sara shrunk back behind him. The vehicle had taken the corner a lot more sedately than the previous one. A very smartly dressed couple appeared from the car. One was a middle-aged man with a very badly fitting toupee, accompanied by a woman with immaculate dress sense, but unfortunately lacking the face to match. The new arrivals entered through the broken doors and disappeared inside. At the same time a noise above Cal and Sara alerted them to the fact that their exit point had been discovered. Footsteps on the stairway were coming down towards their position.

Cal and Sara burst through the door and ran over to the subway entrance. They looked inside but all that was visible was a very murky half-light failing to do its job in cheering the unfortunates who needed to use this connection to the other side of the river. It was more advisable to use the more conventional modes of transport above.

Cal looked over his shoulder and noticed the emergency exit door on their building opening. Without waiting to see what was emerging, Cal took Sara's hand again and pulled her into the subway. Once inside they both halted. The light was not good. They had to let their eyes get used to the dimness. Cal said to the rock, 'Why don't you give us some assistance here? Can't see a thing in this light.' But the little one was not in evidence.

'Typical! Must be a man. I thought for some moment it might be a she. But there you go. Always hoping,' said Sara, shivering.

'Hoping for what, Sara? I was back there looking at their strength. In numbers maybe. But certainly the intellectual level is well short of our combination.'

Cal actually managed a chuckle, but this soon halted as he caught hold of her. Pointing ahead of them, Sara froze.

In the distance a shape loomed towards them. All that could be heard was the dripping of water – some of it loud – in front of their position; and more faintly in the distance further on. The shape came closer still. The light was now sufficient to make out features. A stubbly beard, and white sparkling eyes on a darkened face. A soft voice called to them. 'Not often anyone passes through here anymore. Nice for me. Good night's sleep.' The speaker chuckled, then coughed and spat the contents to the floor. Sara retched silently. 'Just wondered if you kind folks could find it in yourselves to offer this poor unfortunate the price of a cup of coffee. Just a little spare change for a parched soul.'

Sara rummaged through her bag and came out with a handful of change which she handed to Cal, not wanting to approach this person herself. Cal inwardly wasn't that much more confident, but he handed over the coins to the tramp. Then they were off again, rushing past the prone figure of the down-and-out. He farted as they passed. The tramp was still trying to formulate his words of thanks to them, but a couple of minutes later he was being confronted by a completely different set of humanity.

Two of the original suited door-wreckers were now inside the subway facing him, firearms in their hands, pointing in his direction.

'You see a couple go by this way? Young man and woman? Jesus, do you stink!'

The suit was smart but the contents of his head maybe not. He had a broken nose and the general demeanour of a boxer.

'Sorry, mister. Poor diet and all that. Shit myself badly. Think I might have a touch of that fever. Catching shit… you know it?'

The boxer looked at his colleague. 'What's he going on about?'

The other man stepped back from the tramp's position. 'Archie, for fuck's sake. What we doing down here? This fucker has the pox, for fuck's sake. Don't mind dying in a shoot-out but I ain't becoming a stiff out of this lowlife fucker. They didn't come down here. On the train or bus above us. We're wasting valuable time. They will want us to be at their apartments next. Coney and that bitch will be at our throats if they get there before us.'

Both suits left the same way they entered.

The tramp was now rubbing the coins in his hand, chuckling. 'One good turn deserves another. And you, my little friend, better catch up with them!'

Cal and Sara emerged at the other side, breathing a sigh of relief. Cal listened. Nothing. Nobody following. Only the rock appeared, hovering for a second or two and then landing in Cal's hand. He put it in his pocket and they headed for the bus station.

They decided to stake it out for a few minutes. But there were no signs of the chasing mob. They consulted the timetables searching for the number of the bus which would take them nearest to the spot. But feeling just a little panicked, they caught the first bus out in the general direction of the burial point. When they came to alight, the bus driver showed much curiosity. He was scratching his head. 'Are you sure you want to get off here? Not a lot around but rocks – and more rocks.'

Cal countered. 'Nice evening for a stroll. It's just the way we like things.' Sara got off without saying anything. She was now far from convinced about this assignment.

'Okay. Have it as you wish. Perhaps see you both on the return journey.' The driver shut the doors and the bus departed.

Sara asked, 'Where exactly are we? Where is the nearest town?'

Cal frowned. 'Maybe seven, eight miles.'

She went off immediately in the direction of the departing

bus, but was too late to change anything. 'Stop. For fuck's sake, stop!' she cried, but all she received was a mouthful of dust particles.

'You wouldn't really have left me out here on my own?' Cal asked.

Sara, still spitting dust from her mouth, just glared at him. He got the message clear. Taking the rock from his pocket, he held it up in the air. The rock knew the purpose, left his hand and hovered for a second before heading off in the direction of its 'home'.

Sara reluctantly trudged after Cal's moving figure, following the rock's path of light. The rock shone like a flare over the terrain. Unfortunately, the pair still managed to trip and stumble, with too frequent falls. On one of the last occasions, Sara cursed. Cal, hearing this, apologised to his little friend.

'It's alright, little fella. Or you might just be a Miss. Especially in light of the nagging. Sorry. Not my intention to insult, but I seem to be able to do that without much thought. Not on purpose, I mean. Sara is stressed. Bit overstressed, actually. It being her nature to react. Or overreact.'

Sara was now champing at the bit. 'Overstressed. *OVER-FUCKING-STRESSED*! Be careful, Cal. Patronising me is one thing. No, it's everything. Fuck you. I have dished out bloody noses and black eyes in the past. No fucking man ever gave me respect.'

Cal was again regretting opening his mouth. He apologised. 'Sorry, Sara. I am the one who is probably overstressed. Words just come out the wrong way when I'm like this.'

'No *probably* about that – more a certainty! Just learn to think first before opening that trap of yours, Cal.'

Cal found the spot. The little rock hovered over them, illuminating the place. Sara took out the bag of food and drink she had purchased at the bus station. Fortunately, having the presence of mind to realise that it could be a long night. Both sat down on boulders to eat. The rock descended on to Cal's leg, vibrating gently. This gave him a peculiar but pleasant sensation – in fact, very pleasant indeed! It sent a warm glow all the way up to his loins. If only Sara knew. But there again, it might send her in to another temper tantrum. And Cal had no wish to be her next victim!

Cal, having finished his meal, got down on hands and knees. He began to dig a hole, using the plastic knife from his takeaway meal. He found himself suddenly overcome. Tears began to drip into the hole as he dug. Cal couldn't quite understand this sudden emotion. Maybe it reminded him of E. Earth to earth, and all that. The rock plopped itself into the hole in front of Cal, who nodded to it. He began wiping the tears away with the back of his hand.

Sara noticed Cal's upset. It caused a strange sensation in herself. She too felt suddenly very sad. As she had when her dear grandmother had passed away. She turned her back, not wanting Cal to witness her – Sara – shedding a tear.

The rock popped out of the hole again, causing Cal to sit back on his haunches. The rock hovered over the two of them. First to Cal, then to Sara. It shed a shard to each of them from itself, and then returned to the hole. Cal proceeded to fill this in, covering the vibrating object. 'Sleep well, little one,' he whispered.

Afterwards, on the long hike back, the shards illuminated the way. Both of them held their individual 'sparklers' up in the air. These afforded them sufficient light and both managed to get back to the roadway without further mishap. Sara sat down feeling very tired and in need of a bath.

'Oh Cal, I am not cut out for this shit! What are we going to do? If we use our credit cards they will be able to find us. Cal, I am not best pleased.'

Cal looked at Sara. He was grinning, and this confused her. She was about to fly at him but Cal held a calming hand up to her. 'The little man flashed a message on my screen at home advising me before I came to work. Said I was to take all of my money out of my accounts. It's not easy for me to do that. I was brought up to be very careful with my assets.'

Sara looked at him and smirked. 'I've heard it called many things but not an asset!' Cal didn't appear to get the joke but produced a wad of banknotes from his briefcase.

Sara blinked and then screamed with delight. Cal nearly fell off his boulder.

'Cash, wonderful, wonderful cash! Do I feel much better! So

happy. We can get back to town and find a room. A bath or shower. Oh, I am really, *really* relieved. Thank you, Cal. She reached over to him and gave him a hug. Then she kissed him on his cheek. Cal went the colour of beetroot.

In the distance they heard the sound of the bus returning. Same driver, still curious. 'So you folks had a good long walk in the wild? Never issued a return ticket to the wilderness before!'

Cal and Sara found seats without a reply. The driver looked hard at them in his rear-view mirror.

As the bus entered town it stopped for a large crowd. It turned out to be a family outing, and they seemed not best pleased. By all accounts they'd been waiting an hour for the bus to arrive. As the commotion held the driver's attention, Cal and Sara slipped past him off the bus. They could still hear the raised voices when across the street. They walked for a little while then spotted a small motel advertising room vacancies. The receptionist appeared lonely and bored, but the pair were in no mood for small talk.

They booked in as Mr and Mrs Stone! Cal gave a hefty tip with the normal rental, which seemed to do the trick. He hoped so anyway, as they hadn't offered any form of ID, and after the generous overpayment the receptionist did not appear to be requesting any.

Once in the room, Sara dashed to the bathroom and locked herself in! 'Sorry Cal. Needs must!' she shouted through the door.

'No probs here. Going to watch some television – and relax.'

Cal lay on a bed flicking through channels with the remote. By the time Sara emerged from her soak in the shower Cal was watching the news. She padded across the room towards him, wearing a bathrobe. As she reclined on the other bed Cal was sucking in breath.

'What is the matter, Cal?' Sara said, closing her eyes.

'Just look at this,' Cal replied. On the screen were images of persons being handcuffed and led away. The report centred on investigations into bizarre sects who appeared to be collecting asteroid rock and wearing samples about themselves as chalices or charms. To the general public this behaviour would not in itself be cause for concern, but higher members of the sects were being detained in various countries all over the world. It was considered that they may have connections with terrorist organisations.

Cal was incensed. 'Pretty cute. So they arrest these people as they have other groups and lock them away under their flimsy "you are not us" laws.'

'People like us, Cal,' Sara remarked.

Cal looked at her. 'That is exactly what is concerning me now. Those shards of rock. Wearing them about ourselves for protection. But how do they come up with this idea of terrorists?'

'Perhaps it is the only way they can keep the whole thing hushed up. You know, no one is allowed information or proper access when dealing with governments and the war on terrorism. Like you say, pretty cute.' Sara lay back down and closed her eyes again.

'So what do we do now?' Cal asked. 'Just sit tight?'

'I have a feeling we are going to be visited again regarding this mess. But remember, Cal, what we were told. Stay within the truth and we will be protected. Maybe the whole thing is a set-up to draw the other side out. But remember the power and intelligence emitting from that rock. I know whose side I want to be on.'

At this, they were both dazzled when the splinters of rock glowed so brightly the room became a total yellow and green experience!

'There – what more proof do you need, Cal?' A few seconds later Sara drifted into a well-earned sleep.

Cal covered her gently with a blanket. Sara muttered incoherently and pulled the cover around herself turning onto her side at the same time. Cal gazed down on her. She looked to him so beautiful and peaceful; a far cry from the fiery woman she could be. He walked over to the bathroom and was soon himself immersed in water and his many thoughts. Afterwards, he too found a bathrobe and made for his bed. He too was now in need of sleep. But there was to be no sleep yet. Suddenly the door blew in!

Sara awoke with a start and sat bolt upright but still not fully conscious. Cal was frozen to the spot in terror. What the pair were expecting to appear were the likes of the four assassins from the raid on the building. But these forms were not human. Nothing like either of them had ever seen – even in the dodgiest of movies!

Grotesquely malformed, with piercing eyes, jabbering in an indistinguishable manner, half a dozen of these creatures appeared. Slime dripped from their bodies. They began to advance on Cal and Sara, but from nowhere a lightning flash struck all the forms at once, leaving a bundle of burning stinking sludge.

The pair stared at the sight with disbelieving eyes. Then the horrible smell hit them. Both started retching. Cal rushed for an open window. He had to let go and throw up, hoping no one was being inconvenienced below! Sara was gulping but managed to keep everything down.

Cal, reeling with nausea, half turned back towards the pile, just in time to see hooded figures clearing up the mess. All departed in a flash, leaving nothing behind. Even the smell had gone.

From another side of the room a doorway opened into a bright light. The shards also glowed an apparent welcoming as another cloaked figure entered. The soft penetrating voice then entered them as before.

Chapter Four

'Greetings again! Firstly I must apologise for being so lax on this occasion. This will not happen again. It appears, as recent events have indicated, we will have to be more generally vigilant. We are dealing with the nature of a particular beast. Those creatures were the product of many failed esoteric experiments. Being human and mortal has forever been a major headache for their line. There are no lengths they will not go to in order to save themselves. From time to time their leadership has suffered through the death of a certain party. They have then waited long for a replacement birth. What could be more terrifying for humanity? An immortal tribe of this genre. Of course, we have always assisted with their experiments, ensuring failure. It can be very satisfying watching their most eminent scientific brains looking so disillusioned after yet another experiment hits the rocks. But this failure can produce in them an even more sadistic frenzy. We have witnessed so many incidents where terrible things have been meted out to unfortunates not of their own kind. You have now an enormous amount of knowledge. It would be extremely dangerous for you to speak of it to anyone. It would be catastrophic and beyond our protection. Do you understand?'

Both nodded back. 'Good, we are very pleased with you. However, we have next a task which will entail a certain amount of risk to us, but not yourselves. The shards are fully aware of their purpose to you. They ensure your protection whilst conducting affairs under our banner. These will never desert you. Whatever happens, they will find you again if lost or confiscated.'

At this the splinters shone brightly, as if to acknowledge this statement.

'May I ask a question, please?' Cal had raised a hand as if asking a question of a teacher in school.

'Certainly, Calvin. What is your question?'

'We were watching a news programme earlier. It was

mentioning about the arrests of people said to be in strange sects who collected asteroid rock, and then connecting this to terrorism.'

'Ah, Calvin. Not everything is as it seems. It is all part of a larger game plan. For them to actually broadcast this news reveals a major flaw in their strategy. Believe me, they have made huge mistakes. I am not permitted to divulge anything further, but be assured everything is moving forward at last for our line after so long in the wilderness. With your kind assistance we can penetrate even further.'

Sara waved a hand at Cal. 'You see. I said something similar. Drawing them out. Remember?' Cal agreed.

The figure rose slightly, hovering six inches from the ground. 'Your task for us is to locate and obtain a particular ring made of quartz. This is to be placed in your room for me to collect. To achieve this I will have to again pass through a doorway, but this time leaving myself highly vulnerable to attack. If caught it will be my end. But then another of us would arrange a similar exercise until success is achieved. Do not be concerned about the danger to me. The chances of success are in our favour. I only mention it in case something unforeseen occurs.'

Cal's shard left his hand, having been summoned by the figure. An old piece of parchment passed from the figure attaching itself to the splinter of rock. It then returned to Cal, dropping the parchment into his still opened hand. The hood on the cloaked figure rose sufficiently for the pair to see the goldfish bowl again, but the images therein were now of a beautiful woman and child.

'Good fortune with your search. We have narrowed it down to the south side of this city.'

The figure then disappeared leaving Cal looking closely at the parchment.

'Wow! This looks old. Very ancient. But the paper feels quite new. It has the picture of the ring.'

Sara stepped over and took the parchment from him. She too studied it. 'Beautiful. Shouldn't be too hard to spot this.'

The following morning, after experiencing fitful sleep, the pair made their way out of the motel past the reception desk, which was now manned by a different receptionist who merely nodded a good morning. Catching a bus to the south side, they both sat in silence. Nerves now beginning to jangle.

Initial efforts drew a blank. After visiting numerous shops, they increasingly began to feel a desperation previously unknown to them, even in the mundane world of corporate serfdom. But it also brought to the surface a sense of rebelliousness which was to later serve them well, and an inner confidence and sense of purpose. They were learning.

'It's like we are in a film,' Sara remarked, 'in a moment of suspense only meant for real actors – people we are used to watching and wondering how they can be so brilliant all of the time. They always end up saving the day. Where are they in reality?'

Cal nodded his agreement but inside of him he was feeling still a little lost, and it clashed with the new-found inner confidence. But this was Cal's way of dealing with new situations. He was thinking to himself, please let this mean no more dork. No more 'clumsy fucking prick' – as his previous boss had screamed at him in front of the whole office after another of his mishaps.

'Cal... Jesus! Tell me I am hallucinating. There it is. Isn't it? Cal? Cal? *Cal*!' Sara turned towards where he should have been, right at her side. But Cal was several yards behind her, entranced with the view in another shop window – his own reflection! 'Get your ass down here!' Sara hissed at him.

Cal shuddered at the familiar tone. He couldn't help it if he was prone to daydreaming. But didn't offer it as an excuse.

'Did you hear what I said? No! Because as is usual you drift off into another fucking world.'

He winced. 'Sara, you are swearing a little too much, and being aggressive with it.'

'Jesus, I swear I will swear at this fucking idiot until he realises what counts in all of this. Do you hear me, Cal? Keep up with me.' She recounted her original statement, pointing at the object sitting in the jewellery store-front display. Cal peered closely at it. He agreed it looked like the one. Eyes to parchment then back to the displayed ring. Yes, Cal thought, that's the baby. He was suddenly excited again. 'Let's go for it!'

Sara shook her head, looking long and hard at him. 'What really goes on in that mind of yours, Cal? Please keep up with it all. Stop dropping out into your own world. *Please*!'

Cal shrugged. Perhaps Sara was more right than she thought. He just realised he was not really that brave. But he could pretend, maybe.

As the pair entered the shop the proprietor eyed them curiously over spectacles perched on the bridge of his nose. He was clearly Jewish, as many of the previous shop owners had been. But this old guy appeared friendly and open to bargaining. Especially on observing Sara's initial delight from the other side of the pane of glass in his shopfront! He had watched the animated conversation with much amusement, which was one of the reasons his eyes were glittering. To him, they were a normal couple trying to find that engagement ring. Maybe the man was a little nervous, especially of the price. The reason why the lady was giving all the yap, he reckoned.

'Okay, Okay. You young folks want it so badly but I have bills to pay too. Can't give it away, you know. This is definitely worthy of an heirloom. Just look at the quality, the craftsmanship. If I could afford to I would be keeping it for myself, believe me.'

He looked intently at them both. The boy was a giveaway. Sold! If only he had come alone... but the girl was glaring at him. Made him feel very uncomfortable. And there was a strange luminescent glow about her.

Cal noticed this and was grinning. His own shard hadn't connected. But Sara's obviously had a mission! Thank goodness she was here and dealing with it all, Cal thought. I would have definitely been taken for the proverbial sucker.

A price was agreed. At this Sara's features began to soften – in truth, with relief. But the old man was not to know this. He felt a little better, but not quite reassured. Something inside of him was screaming. He just couldn't figure out what exactly it wanted...

The amount agreed was handed over in cash to the now astonished shop owner. 'Haven't had a cash settlement on an amount like this for ages!' He rubbed his hands together before accepting the bundle. He counted it out, holding up to the light every other bill, checking for authenticity. 'Seems to be all here. Sorry for the time I took, though. Can't be too careful. No offence intended,' he said.

'None taken!' Cal replied.

He waved them off the premises but some instinct was telling him he'd been had; that the ring had been extra special. But he just wanted to forget it now and go have a lie-down. He was tired and in need of a rest. That glow about the lady had become more intense as the haggling proceeded. It had made him feel drained. The old guy walked over to the front door turning the 'Open' sign to 'Closed'. He peered out into the street for a final glimpse of the couple, but they had vanished.

In fact, Cal and Sara had both run full pelt away from the shop, around a corner and into an alley. In hindsight, they both realised this to have been an extremely naive reaction. What if the shop proprietor had been quick enough to spot this and had cried out the proverbial 'Stop thief!'? Especially as the old guy hadn't offered them a receipt. Paying cash without anything to back up the transaction, as a credit card bill would have done. It did not bear thinking about!

Back in the motel room the ring was placed on a desktop.

Come the hour, something didn't feel right. An unexplained tension between them; an air of hostility. Cal's hackles were already up, but he wasn't looking for an attack from quite that direction. Suddenly Sara lunged at him, her hands around his neck, beginning to throttle him. Choking, losing his senses, he had just enough left to witness a cloaked and hooded figure pass by. In desperation, Cal raised an arm, pointing fingers over her shoulder in the direction of the figure, but Sara was far gone. Everything went black for Cal as he passed out...

Some moments later he awoke. Head thumping, mouth dry, throat on fire. On seeing Cal coming around, Sara approached with a glass of cool water, which he gulped down, but then coughed most of it back up on to his chest.

'Sorry. Oh Christ, Cal, I am sorry!' Sara appeared inconsolable in her grief. 'How could I have done this? Christ – and the ring has disappeared! What happened to me? I like you, for Christ's sake. Why the hell was I trying to strangle you?'

Cal felt strangely in command of the situation. His head was a beating drum, his tonsils felt like they had been replaced by barbed wire, but an inner sense seemed to take over.

'A diversion, Sara. He, or it, or whatever, appeared at the same time. I had already picked up the ring. It was in my hand when I pointed at the figure. I wanted you to see it but you obviously had something else on your mind!'

'Don't! Cal, I said I'm sorry. Was it them that made me? Diversion, you said. I'm not feeling too good, Cal. The ring, Cal, what happened to the ring?' Sara started to shake. Her face white she was close to collapsing.

Cal reached out, strong arms held her upright. She fell into his embrace, weeping uncontrollably. He laid her down in a comfortable position on the bed.

Whispering gently into her ear, Cal reassured Sara of his notion that all had gone to plan. 'I really sense the ring is with them. It was very important to them. We have been successful. So calm down.' As Cal spoke these words, the shards glowed and came together in their own embrace. Cal watched in disbelief. 'What are they up to, Sara?'

'Cal, you will never find out the meaning of life searching in those fields with your little stick.' Her next reaction both surprised and delighted him. 'This is what the rocks mean.' Her arms reached out, pulling him down. Their lips met. The following hours were a haze for both of them. Hard flesh found soft flesh again and again. Channels swam with future life. Cal and Sara, like their shards, were truly as one!

Chapter Five

Sara awoke to find half of the bed empty. She quickly arose and saw Cal standing by a window staring out on the still dark streets. The illuminated landscape appeared to play tricks on the eyes. A drifting newspaper for a split second took the form of a cat or similar creature. The shadows appeared to hide any manner of potentially dangerous or frightening situations. Was it just his imagination running riot again? *No*. There. Look closely. Movement. And another over there. Not imagining. They are coming for us!

Cal turned quickly, sensing Sara behind him. Grabbing her, he pushed her away from the window just as something thudded against the window. The high velocity bullet pierced the glass with minimal damage and now lay embedded in the wall inches away from Sara's prone position. 'Christ, that was too close for comfort! Let's get out of here.' Cal was already opening the door.

'What, just leave me? I'm not dressed, Cal. I can't just run out there without clothes.' Sara began to dress in haste.

'Trust a woman to think of clothes at a time like this!' Cal gulped back in realising what he had just uttered.

'Sexist pig!' Sara scowled at Cal, but on seeing his extreme discomfort she chuckled, despite the imminent danger. 'The rocks!' But she needn't have worried; they were now as two. Each had found its human partner. Both felt an overwhelming sense of calm as they glowed in their hands. They needed that serenity, for the hotel room was about to be trashed.

As the intruders entered the room, Cal held his shard up towards them. Sara followed suit. The suits froze. Automatic weapons dropped from their hands to floor. All four of them remained static, unmoving. Sara and Cal took the opportunity to by-pass the stationary figures, Cal cheekily giving one of them a light slap on his the face as he passed by.

'Cal, be careful – that could just wake him up,' Sara said

disapprovingly. Back to her usual self, she was glaring at him intensively. But Cal was now feeling in a devilish mood and stood his ground. He studied the men, then looked at the rocks still glowing brightly.

'No, Sara, they're out for the count. These little babies are the absolute real thing.' The shards shone ever brighter. 'When are we going to wake up from all this? It's not real – can't be real.'

'It's real alright, Cal. Just get yourself moving out of here, before we run out of juice or whatever these – *your* – babies run on.' Sara sensed she might have gone a little too far this time but Cal was sanguine in reply.

'They are not light bulbs, dear. They are luminous magical rock...' Cal started to explain.

'Just shut up! Don't patronise me or I will throttle you properly this time.' Sara chuckled again, pleased with where that came from! 'But why am I laughing? I'm bloody angry, but what the hell. These little friends do weird and wonderful things for us, eh, Cal? Cal?'

She looked about her. He had disappeared. Sara gingerly stepped back into the room. Grabbing her bag and Cal's briefcase, she exited. As she stepped outside the door, Sara found the night shift receptionist standing like a statue by the stairway. She gave him a hefty kick in the privates. He wouldn't enjoy the wake-up call!

Sara stood shivering in the shadows of a run-down building, catching back her breath after running for some distance. The building had once housed a thriving industry but now bore all the familiar signs of decay. An institution no longer required in this modern progressive world. A workforce now bereft and seeking opportunities elsewhere. If they could be accepted, that is. For many of them too late. Another layer for the scrap heap.

'Where the hell is he?' she gasped between short breaths. Not trying to feel scared. 'How did he vanish like that? I was only giving small talk in the form of a bollocking. Where was the harm in that? After all, we are a couple now, aren't we? Nothing makes sense anymore.' Sara was having grave doubts. A brief flash, however, startled her back to the present. And there stood Cal.

'Don't ask. I don't know either. One moment I was with you,

then I was whisked away. I could see you but it was if I was in an alternate space. Calling to you, but you were obviously unable to hear me. Weird.'

Sara glared. 'Perhaps the shard agreed with me and got you out of there before you got us in to a lot more danger. Cal, it is not a game, you know. These rocks are trying to protect us and you play around like that...' Cal's shard suddenly left him and flew over to Sara, joining her own... 'There – it's been confiscated until you grow up!'

Cal looked sheepish. Looking down, he stared at his feet. 'Sorry,' he muttered.

Sara swallowed. 'But at least you are back in one piece. And I am relieved at that. After all, I might just be having our baby. So you had better grow up overnight, buster. Lots of responsibility coming your way.'

Cal began to grin but this was cut short. Sara began to sob. Tears rolled down her reddened cheeks. 'What is happening to me? I'm not usually so dramatic.'

Cal hugged her. She wanted to pull away but allowed him to all the same. And anyway, it felt good. He said, 'Perhaps we have to learn to live with what is happening to us. All for a purpose.'

'You are starting that patronising again, Cal. I don't ever do patronising.' She pushed him away from herself and ducked back in to the shadows, suddenly aware again of their fugitive status. She looked furtively around her.

Cal removed his glasses, rubbing his eyes and ever so slightly shaking his head. He didn't want Sara to notice in case it set her off again. Then he joined her in the gloom.

The pair eventually found another motel. Again they went going through the same procedures including the tip; but neither, after the previous experience, were holding out much hope. They were expecting a repeat performance.

During that night both of them had dreams. Clear and vivid. The cloaked figure had returned, thanking them for their brave efforts. That the ring was now back with the true one. And she was eternally grateful.

The next morning Cal interrupted Sara telling her version of the dream. 'What did you say about capture?' he asked.

'We are to let ourselves be taken in for questioning. It is our next task.' Sara didn't appear to be perturbed.

'You don't seem to mind,' said Cal. 'It didn't feature in my dream. Why?' He considered this for a moment.

'Maybe you missed it,' said Sara.

'Wouldn't have missed something as important and scary as voluntarily giving up my liberty. Especially to those goons. No way do I want to do that. Count me out.' Cal slumped down into the chair, his head in his hands.

Sara was just about to give Cal another piece of her mind, but before she could utter a word of vehemence the door suddenly blew open. Cal looked up, eyes wide. 'Not again. *Jesus, we're trapped!*' Worse still, the shards both exited out of the open window.

'Freeze you terrorist-supporting fuckshits!'

It seemed the whole doorway was jammed full of firearms. Orders were being barked for the pair to lie on the floor, hands behind heads. Both were then frisked in most harsh terms.

'*Ow*! You pig – that hurt! What makes you think I would conceal anything there? You're just a fucking pervert.' Sara felt a blow to the back of her head.

'Shut the fuck up, terrorist bitch. On your feet. You got some explaining to do. Gave us the slip a couple of times, but you're not going to get away this time, huh? Mind you, your idiot boyfriend seems a lot tamer than you.'

Sara staggered as she was pulled to her feet, still reeling from the blow. The back of her neck felt damp. Bleeding, she presumed. She was plenty angry.

'Bet he's the one who ends up tied to the bedstead as you fuck him, huh?'

All the suits and officers chuckled at this. The one holding Sara was about to continue the abuse but as he stepped in front of her she summoned up all her remaining strength, kneeing the officer in the groin square on. It hurt! He went down, groaning, on all fours.

A suit – the 'boxer', in fact – went to pistol whip Sara but Cal was able to free himself from his captor and halt the intended blow. Surprised by his action, he followed it up by delivering a massive blow to the suit's back, sending him flying across the room into a solid collision with a wall. Blood spurted from the wound on his forehead which had taken the brunt of the forced impact. The now unconscious suit's face scraped down the wall, breaking his nose again noisily as his body collapsed into a heap.

Sara clapped her hands, eyes shining in admiration at her newfound knight with shining 'armour'!

Both were then, not unexpectedly, dumped on the floor. Handcuffs being applied to wrists held behind them with brutish force, causing the pair to cry out in pain. But this was immediately silenced by a bark of 'Shut the fuck up!', backed up with weapons cocked and held at their temples. Eyes now tightly shut, they waited for the explosion. The officers were seemingly too pissed off to care about the consequences.

The explosion came, but from the doorway. Verbal, not gunshot.

'Any of you fuckers pull those triggers, and I assure you a lifetime amongst my friends on "A" block at the local madhouse. Who put you incompetent shits in on our operation anyway?'

Before anyone could reply the voice boomed again – deep, rich and definitely black!

'Out, out, out, you motherfuckers!'

The room began to empty as quickly as it had been entered. They dragged the unconscious suited 'boxer', leaving a trail of blood behind him. Another was assisting the still groaning limp lump of uniform who held tightly to his privates. He watched them pass with a withering look of disdain.

Sara and Cal looked up best they could from their prone positions in the direction of the doorway. *He* was tall, proportionate in build. Dark-skinned; very dark. Scars, deeply etched in his cheeks. Tribal. This was one mean-looking Blackman. Suited. In fact, a very well-cut affair, but did not look quite right on this man. Would have looked more in place dressed as a voodoo priest at ceremony. Cal considered this. He was into such things. Not doing, but some of the objects he collected were used in such ceremonies. Cal had a real curiosity about the whole thing. Perhaps just a little overcurious!

The eyes, dark and menacing, bored into the pair. Sara just stared back. *That* stare. Defiance. The Blackman smiled back at her and she looked away.

He spoke again, this time low, surprisingly soft given his entrance speech. It reminded them both of...

'Some of my line have connected with you, I know. I am the one they speak of in your dreamtime. The reason for your capture was to connect with me. But something has gone wrong. The shards left you unprotected and you have been injured. I will get to the bottom of this.' He knelt down and undid the handcuffs, helping first Sara, then Cal, to their feet. He ushered them to sit.

The shards reappeared through the window. They hovered, waiting for instruction. The Blackman held out his hands to them and they both glowed as each dropped into a palm. 'I will be taking these in for questioning. They are still your protectors, but that protection is now in my jurisdiction until further notice. My line has obviously been compromised, possibly even infiltrated. They will not rest until it is resolved. There will be no stone left unturned.'

The pair then looked past him. All those who had been leaving were now motionless in the hallway. The Blackman noticed their obvious surprise. 'As you have experienced yourselves, the shards have the same power. I may just be a little more powerful.' He chuckled. 'My name is *Gordon*. Donald Gordon. A strange name for a Blackman, I know. Long story. Maybe another time. Well, introductions over, Calvin and Sara, I must have you also accompany me to the offices of my affairs. Which is a local police station on this occasion. There I will speak to you more when I have finished with the rocks here. Do not worry. They have done nothing wrong. Only follow instructions given them. Something made them decamp at a vital time.' Gordon looked down. He was considering the situation. Then he nodded to himself.

'The shards have just given a general insight into why you were chosen. You see, I am the difficult one as far as my line are concerned. They have appealed to me before, but I have an immense responsibility to those who have followed me through my many existences. You have already been advised how what cannot be seen is not necessarily not there?'

Both nodded.

'Most in this world scoff at such a suggestion. The irony is, the majority of your peoples are fed the fact of such non-existence by the few who know, as we do, the reality beyond. But they are not us. They have a plan for themselves which requires everyone else to live in ignorance. It is the only way their plan will work. Perhaps!' Again Gordon chuckled. 'You think that nature just makes the wind to blow in your hair? But how many armies ride unseen on such a phenomenon as a hurricane? A typhoon? Tornado? Unfortunately, many of those I wish to save are trapped here, and my line cannot, for complicated reasons, ensure the safe passage of all those I wish to accompany me back. Therefore, I would at this time rather remain with them and suffer what is to be. Take my chances alongside them, as they have in the past with me. In this world I have been amongst many bad people. Terrifying people. Betrayal is second nature to them. That is why I value the true friends I have around me. For all of us it has been a nightmare. We will see it through to the end together. Enough of this talk. Now we must go through the formalities. Arrest and interrogation and all that. But do not worry, I will be close at hand. I know you both have questions, but I will ask you please do direct them at me later. Is that alright?'

Both again nodded. Secretly, they were still in shock but had managed to take in most of what he had said.

As he turned towards the door the authoritarian raiding party began to move again. One or two glanced back at him making them move that little bit faster, spurring on the rest of the ensemble. They looked a sorry sight!

A couple more suits came through the door and took the pair to a waiting limo. At least the cuffs were off. Neither Cal nor Sara felt like conversation though. At the police station they were dumped in a room together. Sitting side by side at a table, with two empty chairs on the other side facing them.

Cal broke their silence, whispering to Sara, 'I know the shards did a job on those goons. But what that Donald Gordon did was something else. While he was talking to us all those jackass sons of bitches were suspended animation projects.'

Sara merely nodded. She was still feeling dazed and a little sick. She was also more than a little put out that Gordon had not arranged for her wound to be attended to. As she was thinking this, a suit carrying a medical bag entered the room. Introducing himself as the local police doctor, he proceeded to tend to the head wound. Sara was less than impressed when he wanted to wrap a bandage around her head, but finally she agreed after much persuasion from both Cal and the doctor.

Sara was now feeling a little more like herself. She had been worrying about the extent of her injury and now felt reassured it hadn't been as bad as she had first thought. The gun had grazed her scalp rather then cut or indenting it.

'Cal, you asked me earlier what I thought of what the Blackman did. This is not what I am good at – spooks and the like. Anything in this world I'll stand up to and kick in the balls when I get a chance, if it pisses me off. But all this other stuff is way above my head. Especially him talking about his "other lives" and his "invisible armies".' Cal chuckled. 'It's not funny, Cal. I am deadly serious.' Sara was not amused.

'No, no, I'm not laughing at your fear of spooks. You were saying about kicking people in the balls if they piss you off.'

'Bastard deserved it! Pity I hadn't hobnails on. Make a real good job!'

'I'd say you did okay without them.' Cal chuckled again at the memory.

'Anyway, Cal, what about your sudden elevation to superhero?'

Cal mimicked a bashful look. 'Aw shucks, Olive.'

Sara kicked him under the table. 'Are you saying because I am slender I look like Popeye's Olive?'

Cal look horrified, and was about to launch into another speech on Sara's sensitivity over personal remarks when he caught her smirking. They both chuckled.

'Finding something funny, are we?' Both of them were startled and sat bolt upright.

Two different suits entered the room. Male and female. Both looking at their watches. They sat down opposite Cal and Sara.

The man was fifty, maybe, balding with tight toupee. Plus the usual problem around the gut. No piece to cover that up! She was a real dresser. Very smart white suit. Expensive hairdo. Solid all-round makeover. Shame about the face, though. Sara's quick summing-up of the pair. She would give her assessment to Cal later.

Neither suit bothered to introduce themselves. A further insult, Sara reckoned which would not go unpunished! The man looked just slightly uncomfortable, Cal thought. But the woman looked a right hard-nosed bitch. Ugly and fierce in equal quantities. Her hostile penetrating eyes rested on each of them in turn. She glared at Sara as if she could read her thoughts about her appearance. Or was the ferocity all show, and really under all that she was a shy, meek home-seeking type? Sara smiled back at her, but Cal looked down.

Cal was now considering two things. There was a man and woman who'd turned up at their work. Yes. These two could well fit that bill. And secondly, that voice. Donald Gordon. The tramp in the subway. No... too far-fetched. But about these two. Be careful what you say, Cal. Got to find a way to alert Sara.

Whilst the woman was doing her utmost to unsettle the pair, the man just merely glanced at them both and then stared into space, watching the smoke rings rise from his cigarette to ceiling.

'Good cop, bad cop,' Cal thought out loud. Then he immediately covered his mouth as if to imply that he hadn't meant to say what he had.

'Come again, young man? Got something to say, have we?' The woman spat this out, diverting her glare from Sara to him. Seeing this, Sara looked enquiringly at Cal.

But he was still trying in his own haphazard way to relay the facts to Sara. 'I've been known to come again. Haven't I, Sara?'

Sara winced, shaking her head violently at him.

'Don't wish to get into your sex life, young man. Nothing you could say on that score would impress this lady. Is that not right, George?'

The man nearly fell out of his chair. 'Yes, Maddie. Of course.'

Sara was starting to bristle. 'What right have you to do this to us?'

The man looked coolly at her before replying, 'I suppose it hasn't crossed either of your minds that we know what you are up to.'

'Like what?' Sara replied defiantly.

'Like shards of quartz. A quartz ring. Strange goings-on. Very strange...' The man blew another puff of smoke at the ceiling.

'Beats me,' Sara said, now staring back at the woman. 'Maddie. Is that spelt like as in *Mad?*'

The woman glanced over at the toupee'd wonder, glaring at him. 'Thanks, George. Please don't use my nickname in front of scum again.'

He visibly winced. 'Sorry, Margaret. Point taken.'

She then turned her glare back to Sara. 'Think we will have to strip-search this little baby. Nothing that makes sense to us coming out of this end, so we will have to examine the other.' The woman hissed the last three words again: *'Examine the other!'*

'Like on your bike, lady! No fucking way are you going anywhere near my end. You pay the local lesbian dive or whorehouse a visit for your jollies and see if there are any takers. Me-thinks your face would be mistaken for a cow's ass.'

Cal gave an involuntary shudder. 'Sara – your language!'

Sara shot a look back at him which he was really glad wasn't loaded. 'Don't patronise me, Cal. Especially after discussing our sex life with these two fucking morons.' Then she hissed, *'Just give me an opening and I'll duff that bitch!'*

Cal thought it was time. 'These two fuckers. Erm, yes, *fuckers*, were the two who arrived at our work. Remember?' Cal was now feeling he'd accomplished something until he looked across at the woman. She was now on her feet. She was ready to pounce at Sara over the insults. But the man had already reacted to the situation with a calming hand on the woman's shoulder. Sara had at last got Cal's drift. She nodded her understanding of this to him.

He looked at the both of them with a faint smile. 'You two lovebirds sorted yourselves out yet? Enough of your bickering, already. This is a serious matter. You could both end up seriously dead. Very dead indeed. We want answers.'

The woman was again glaring at Cal. He removed his glasses and rubbed his eyes. He left the glasses off, placing them gently on the table, and resumed the mutual stare. Hoping she wasn't aware of his short-sightedness. All he could make out was the shape of her head, and he hoped his stare was more or less accurately reflected.

The man cleared his throat. 'Well, Mr Tulley – Calvin, if I may call you that. Seems we got off on the wrong foot earlier.

Certainly, two of our number think so. One has a badly fractured nose and the other, well, put it this way, the medical staff at the hospital are still searching for his balls.'

'Cal, don't listen to that patronising fucker. Anyway, he might not have had any to begin with,' Sara snorted. 'Plenty of mouth to make up for it, though.'

The woman began to rise from her chair again and the man cut in. 'Hey, hey, Margaret – calm it down! Not professional, huh? Getting to you already, and we haven't begun yet.' She resumed her seat. But if looks could kill.

He continued. 'You two, I want no more flippancy or I will let the restraints off my companion here.' He smirked at Margaret's obvious frustration and discomfort. Something told them both he might not be joking.

'We wouldn't want to worry you both overmuch, but another member of your group fucked around during an earlier interview and he is now sitting in a cell with Big Joe. Big Joe, you might ask? Well, little lady and you fella, he's got a root which could have been cut from an oak tree. And he just loves ass. That poor sap should just have stuck to answering our questions in a proper fashion. Now he has got Joe rooting for him. Hah! Geddit? Hah! Now, you wanted to say something, Margaret?'

He sat back with a well-satisfied look on his face. Obviously, delighted with his performance and perfect punch line.

'You're wasted in this job. You should get yourself into cabaret at the local YMCA!' Margaret retorted, now seeing him openly deflate, the smugness evaporating. His face was contorted but still trying to keep a self-appreciating smile.

Margaret stared at Cal and Sara again. Her glare intensified. 'Well, young lady, does the thought of Big Joe enthral you?'

Sara returned the look with a fixed smile on her face. 'Can't tell. Can you recommend him, or is that just the way you normally squat?'

Margaret was on her feet again. 'You sassy bitch! I'll make certain you—'

The door flew open. The interrogators froze.

'Who put Michael in with Joe?' A simple question, but neither seemed to want to answer. The colour went out of their cheeks.

Standing in the doorway again. Same authoritative booming voice. The suited Blackman, Don Gordon, had returned. Just in the nick of time for them. Both were more than grateful to see him, not really appreciating how much.

His scowl took on a sinister, menacing look. The scars appeared to vibrate as he sucked his cheeks in. 'Well? Waiting for an answer here. Not going to wait a lot longer.'

'He – um – he was – um… giving us plenty of lip. Too much. Much to much.' Margaret finally got the words out at a stutter.

Emboldened by his partner, the man joined in. 'Yeah. Much too clever for his own good.'

'That is as maybe, George. But I gave orders for him not to be molested in any way. And what do you two do? Put him in with *the* all-time molester. A fucking fruit, huh?' His eyes were boring into the pair.

'Mr Gordon, I don't think you should take that kind of line, especially in front of prisoners.' The woman was regaining her steely attitude.

'Is that so, Maddie?' He waited for her reaction, which was predictable. But then again, he knew that.

'I have already just warned George over the use of my nickname. I would appreciate you addressing me as Margaret. Is that too much to ask?'

Gordon looked closely at the pair. He had been in another room eavesdropping on the conversation. That was how he knew how to wind Margaret up.

'Then I suppose "Maddie the mad cow" as a fuller version is definitely out?'

Margaret let out a silent scream. She was close to fully losing her composure. Especially given the fact of Sara's bellowing laugh! George noticed Margaret was about to burst and was on his feet with hands on her shoulders. He spat back, 'What the fuck is this all about, Gordon?'

'Ah well, as I seem to have the full attention of both of you… For your information, Michael is not going to be backchatting you, or anyone else; not any more. You see, Joe, being Joe, got a little carried away. Trifle overexcited and strangled our Michael. I say our Michael, as in *our* fucking side. He was undercover.

Wanted it to look absolutely authentic. You know how long he's been amongst that rabble. Huh? Huh?'

They were both gulping dry air as Gordon walked closer to them. He leant over Cal's seated position and thrust another 'Huh'? into the faces of each interrogator.

He then turned back heading for the door but then suddenly spun around, catching the pair exchanging glances. 'Well you might look at each other! Fucking mess you've made now. You know how much that man knew? Of course not. Well, if either of you two can get an answer from him now, this goddamn nigger am gonna go drop his pants in Dixie!'

George and Margaret were now completely devoid of colour. Jaws slack. Vacant expressions. Then Sara noticed that Gordon had turned his back again. Taking a handkerchief from his top pocket he was wiping his face. He spoke again, still with back turned.

'Michael and me, we went back some ways. Like a brother to me. Taking this personally. That is a warning. Do you hear?' Gordon turned. His face streamed with tears. The glare was watery. 'If I find an ulterior motive for Michael's death I will hunt that fucker down for all eternity. Do you understand? *Well, do you?*'

Both interrogators were now shaking slightly, which amused Cal and Sara. This did not go unnoticed, but nothing could be done about it as their ground was long gone, replaced by the unsteadiness of this potential earthquake called Donald Gordon.

'I think I will conduct this interview myself. Maybe you don't agree?' Neither made a move or sound.

'I mean, this molestation thing. Might it be catching, and these two folks are the next in line for a dose?' Gordon moved sideways beyond the door frame. George and Margaret got the message. Both rose in perfect unison and departed through the door, eyes cast downwards.

As Gordon approached Cal and Sara they noticed beyond the doorway two motionless figures. He had done it again!

'Well, you two, it's your turn to ask the questions. But first may I congratulate you both on your demeanour during this recent interview.'

'You were there listening?' Cal asked.

'Of course. I did say to you I would be close. I do not trust those two, even though supposedly they are on our side. Well, they could never be on *my* side. Perhaps they are not on anyone's side but their own. But that is confusing the situation. I do it on purpose sometimes. Confuse the situation, that is. Just my way. But back to you two: well done. Especially impressed with their injuries. They still can't find his balls.' He chuckled.

'Like I said to the other creeps. Maybe he didn't have them in the first place,' said Sara, and Gordon laughed heartily at her response.

Cal was beginning to feel unsure about the Blackman and asked, 'Then whose side are you really on? I heard you telling us earlier of your many armies and friends who are in the beyond. But what about here? As me and Sara are?'

'So say what you are really thinking, Cal. I mean, if Sara keeps going around negating every male's ability to reproduce, the world will have a saviour!'

'He's playing with us, Sara. This guy could fry us if he really concentrated. We are nothing to him. I have read all about those hexes, voodoo and stuff. Scary, very, very scary.' Cal was shaking. He muttered, 'What's getting into me. Why can't I shut the fuck up?'

'Calvin, Calvin. It's your imagination! But I know your fears. Share them if you would, but just let me. You are an overimaginative soul. But without that imagination the magic could not stretch you further. And you need to be stretched, believe me, Calvin. There's lots more to learn, Calvin. A whole lot more. I sometimes feel at bursting point holding on to what I know. But that is my cross to bear. And you, Sara. Feisty and free. World to discover. But maybe not all the world, Sara. Maybe, the freedom is going south too!'

Sara immediately bristled as she was wont to at this suggestion. 'What do you mean, going south? That's usually meant to be directed at a woman's specials as she slips into old age.'

Gordon laughed again at Sara's unique approach to any given situation. 'Yes, it does, when the breasts unfortunately fail to no longer defy gravity. But in your case my meaning is in relation to your impending state of motherhood!'

Cal gulped. 'You can tell that by just looking at her?'

Gordon just stared at Cal until Sara diverted his attention back to herself. 'Well, can you tell? This isn't the normal way of discovery. Tests and doctors' visits and the like. Or is this more of your mumbo-jumbo?'

'You both have still much to learn about the magic. Natural magic, that is. From that source all kinds of perversions have been diverted and established. What you, Cal, call voodoo. There is a bad practice of it by the ignorant. It usually catches up with them in time and takes payment of what it is owed from their souls. Some occasions the soul hasn't enough to make sufficient reparation and is left owing. Hell hath no fury than bad magic spurned! But Calvin, it can and should only be used as nature intended. But I am going too deeply into it for you two to grasp properly. Sufficient to say I can call on my power to assess certain situations. The magic will only work like this if it is treated with the respect it deserves. And yes, you are pregnant, Sara.'

Sara gasped. 'I am still going to get a proper opinion.'

Gordon answered, 'As you wish.'

But Sara hadn't finished. 'I do wish. And I am beginning to wish I had never got caught up in all of this. It is turning into a nightmare. Chased about like fugitives. Manhandled. Beaten up so I have to wear this bloody bandage like a bandanna. And on top of all this I might be pregnant. *Great!*'

Cal stepped towards her. 'I thought you were pleased you might be having our baby.'

Sara shot a look back at him which stopped him in his tracks. 'Cal, for just once, please shut up. I am still in fucking shock.'

'So. You do know why you are here in front of me? I mean it was explained to you, the plan of action?'

Neither of them replied.

'You are aware, are you not? Something must have been said to you about how to approach me on this subject?'

Both gave a head movement to the negative.

'Ha! Very remiss of my brothers. I could just turn and leave now. Leave you with your shards. Which may, or may not, still have the protective qualities they had. I must say I do have grave doubts about that. Especially after what they told me. But you have my curiosity. You are certainly very unusual human beings, so I can see why you were chosen.'

'Perhaps, sir, we represent a certain percentage of our population. Good ordinary citizens who care about things. Want them put right,' Cal ventured.

Sara looked puzzled. 'Cal, why are you calling him, "sir"?'

It was Cal's turn to look a little bemused. 'Did I? Just came out, then. I don't recall. Maybe shows my subservience surfacing. Usually does when I feel this stressed. Usually it's a boss who causes it anyway. So "sir" comes out instinctively.'

'But Calvin, I am not your boss. And I do agree on this point with Sara. So please drop the "sir". Are you sure you were not given more to go on?' Gordon asked.

'We were told not to say anything about it to anyone, or it would be extremely dangerous,' Cal said.

'But I am not just anyone. I *am* their line. The ones you were approached by. The rock you found, Calvin. The ring you rescued. All connected.' Gordon looked at them. Cal and Sara were looking at each other, silently trying to agree on the next move.

Sara eventually said, 'I think he has a point. But I wouldn't say too much yet. Just tell him about the rock heading this way.'

Cal nodded. 'This guy, or whatever, in a hood and cloak with a goldfish bowl for a head asked for our help. Buried the rock again. It gave us the shards. Got the ring from that shop, and the weird guy came back and took it. Also said the world was threatened by what we call an asteroid. But they called it a special name. What was it called now?'

'*Dargumba*, or something like that,' Sara ventured.

'Yes, that's it. *Dargumbastone*. That's what they called it. It's gonna destroy or capture this world. Right, Sara?'

'*Djumbolastone*. Hmm. Interesting.' Gordon looked thoughtful for a moment.

'It means something to you? That name?' Cal asked.

Donald Gordon leant against the door frame. He produced a huge grin. The pair were staring back at him in bemusement. He

55

noticed their questioning looks and tapped his teeth. 'Grandma made these for me. My rightful rotten yellowing tusks am in the freezer back home, boss!'

Cal and Sara sat stunned for a second or two. Then both burst out laughing.

'That's better!' Gordon said, nodding. 'I have been accused in the past of taking myself too seriously. Especially back home. You have caused in me a need to lighten up. My woman would applaud you both for that, I am certain.'

Sara was now very curious. 'And your woman – what planet is she from?'

It was Don Gordon's turn to laugh. 'You, Sara. You have understood something only another female could. You already know I am not from around here. Are you ready for a further truth? I know you are still afraid of – what do you call us?'

Sara was warming to the subject. '*Spooks.*'

'Ah yes, spooks. Allow me a word.' He then opened a line allowing a conversation between Sara and her grandmother. Afterwards, returning to consciousness, Sara, still in shock sat quite still. Cal tried to rouse her with a few words, but she remained in a world of her own choosing.

'What have you done to her? I can't wake her,' Cal said, diverting his attention to the Blackman.

Gordon could sense Cal was becoming annoyed and calmed him. 'Sara is fine. Trust me on that. Do you trust me, Calvin?'

Cal thought about this question for a few seconds. He was feeling very confused, but his inner self was crying out a positive *yes*. He nodded back to Gordon.

'Good. I am very relieved on that score because I want you to join Sara in her state. This is so you will be both relaxed and receptive enough to take in what I am about tell you. But I need your consent, Calvin. For the both of you. It is most important you realise that your mind and Sara's are your own territory. As with land disputes over trespassing, minds too can be subjects of the same. All I am asking for is permission to enter your lands. Have I confused you with my explanation?'

'No. I have followed that bit. It's a good comparison. Land and minds. Trespass. I like that. The subliminal in adverts and the like. Invading our territory. Wow! I could talk with you for hours on this.' Cal was really excited now.

'Maybe find some time later, Calvin. But for now I will put you in with Sara. Okay?'

Cal nodded a 'yes' back at Gordon. 'Fine. Please close your eyes, Calvin.' As he did so, his head tilted slightly and he joined Sara – now in a world of both their choosing!

Chapter Six

'I am *Djumbola*. Priest of *all*. *They* came and slaughtered. The world you reside in is the result. My line, in the past, rarely turned their heads towards this abomination. But slowly their attention has been drawn by my antics and actions. At first they considered me to be an extreme problem. But eventually they must have realised my intentions. Much of it has conflicted with their own considerations. But my recent successes have won over many, even some who had been extremely critical of me in the past. Now they require me to return. But as I have already mentioned to you, this option is not possible without my being able to bring the rest.

However, I am in debt to the magic. Nature requires of me to be its ambassador. So in the final equation my wants and needs are secondary to nature's own requirements. To know magic, an individual must first sense the right path amongst many. The magic gives us all a chance, but the puzzle it presents is like no other in comprehension. Some of its ideas conflict; change at the drop of a hat. This is to be expected, as nothing in the whole ever stands still. Fluctuations in the magical web require counteractions. Nature is basically self-regulatory. But from time to time it requires assistance. Especially in view of the catastrophic occurrences caused by some of this world's inhabitants. That is the particular task I have been set: to attempt to prevent any further disturbances. It is for each individual to follow the path once discovered. But before that discovery, it can involve many wrong paths leading to much pain, frustration and heartache. The obstacles are not always clear. I made many mistakes on my own journey before finding the correct path.

The magic owes nothing to any entity. *All* is preserved by that fact.

Much is passed between each entity during dreamtimes, as you are discovering now; a much practised method of communication, as ancient as time itself. But in this modern world your natural senses have been replaced by high-tech gadgets, producing thinking for you instead of your own thoughts. Your minds become incapacitated – slaves to a culture of mass trespass, eh, Calvin?'

Cal twitched slightly.

'But not all is lost. There are still some who practise the old ways, even though the weight of public opinion is forced against them. Deriding, belittling, abusing those who follow nature's natural ways. Native aboriginal inhabitants and indigenous tribes, for instance. But are they not living the same dreamtime existences as other forms of nature, such as whales and dolphins?

'Now I will take you on a journey of some of my own personal experiences. First witness my slaughter as the Priest *Djumbola* – an untimely death of which I was to suffer at the hands of the same line on numerous occasions. I made my first mistake at this point, uttering curses as I lay dying. Saying forbidden words which allowed my executioners access to nature and the *All*. But unknown to them there are built-in safeguards. Remember, nature is self-regulatory. Without such knowledge fools rush towards a false paradise. Which is exactly how my line view this world.

'I take you now to some of my graves. In Samaria, where I was dispatched with poison by a jealous cousin. To Egypt, where my bones lie beneath a pyramid. On to Damascus, where I often return, feeling my presence there is always welcome. Over the steppes, a Khan of the mighty Mongol Empire. Then there is a site of a burning at the stake in France, as a Knight Templar, no longer valued by King and Pope. These were to follow me soon after. A curse uttered in my final moments before the flames consumed me.

'Close to my heart now: Native American Indian. I would, like many others, never accept the White Man's word. But unfortunately, others did, and we all perished under agonising conditions as treaty after treaty was broken. I still cry with the remembering. Stark memories of my slain brothers and sisters, whole families wiped out – for what? Futuristic hamburger joints, oil for pollution, lands for desecration. The greed and dishonesty of those white men will forever haunt them. That I promise.

'Central America now: Mayan priest. Many questions being asked about my race and what occurred. But would it make any difference if the truth were uncovered? We will have to see.

'Finally Africa. Slavery. West Indies. Voodoo. America. Slavery. Slavers, a curse on you all! Too painful to continue. So many. So many. Too many.'

Cal and Sara blinked back into consciousness. Both their faces were puffy and wet, with tears streaming down cheeks. Realising their state, each felt embarrassed, but this became secondary when looking over to the doorway.

A shaking form. Nude. Eyes wide open. Chanting quietly in a deep whisper. Words indistinguishable.

Sara gasped at the sight, but Cal quietened her. 'He's still there. Wherever it is. Can't wake him. Got to come back himself. Otherwise so dangerous.' This was within Cal's field of knowledge. It made him feel quite assertive.

'Dangerous for who?' Sara whispered.

'All of us!'

Then they both felt an hour skip a beat.

He looked up at them from his crouched position. Wiping his face again with the handkerchief plucked from the top pocket of his now crumpled jacket. Don Gordon was now back rising to his feet. He composed himself.

'I apologise for my loss of demeanour. I meant merely to give you an insight into the workings of nature and her magic, and why I can be so difficult to deal with. Please forgive my lapse. Perhaps I went a little far and too deep. Even for myself.'

Cal spoke. 'It was a wonderful experience. I can see why they want you back. Not just there, wherever there is, but here too. To stay here with them. I felt the warmth of those you were close to. Is that possible – for me to have felt that?'

'It is why you were chosen, Calvin.'

Cal looked down, stifling another tear. Still remembering what he had witnessed, and feeling honoured.

'And you, Sara. What are your considerations?' He looked directly into her eyes. But he was emitting warmth, not the usual glare. Sara blinked furiously, feeling extremely agitated. She stuttered then stopped. Composing herself, she began an attempt at a response.

'I–I – just can't. I'm afraid... of all this. There is no life after death. My mum chided me when I said I could speak to grandma. No, more than that... she frightened the wits out of me. Said it was really a ghost pretending to be her, reacting to my vulnerability, and would whisk me away one night. I really missed grandma when she died. I lay there on the bed sobbing for hours. Then I heard her voice. How confusing is that for a four-year-old? Then your mum saying you were the next offering for Halloween.'

Sara began to sob. Real streaming tears. She felt more embarrassment and did not want to be in this room anymore. She went to get up, without realising that she had not fully recovered. She involuntarily sat back down in her chair with a bump. Cal was now on his feet, but Sara shrugged away his proffered hand of comfort.

'It's okay, Sara. It will take some more time for your confidence to grow. It will, eventually. If it is any comfort, there are so many more out there who have shared similar experiences, when still young, as you have. More than you could ever imagine. But your mother represents a major blocking factor, which is a real problem. So many pass on their own prejudices to their kids, even if, secretly, they actually believe in them themselves.'

'What, you mean my mum might have been frightened like I was? But that was my dear grandma.' Sara frowned.

'Then all I can suggest is next time you converse with her you ask her about it. Maybe it is a factor in why she has come back to you so strongly. Maybe she feels guilty about your mother.' Gordon's eyes were still full of kindness.

'Wait. You said I was pregnant. And if you could tell that you also know the truth about mum and grandma. Is that so?' Sara was getting agitated again.

'I was hoping you wouldn't ask me that. I wanted you to find out from your grandmother. And I still do think it is a matter between you. Everyone makes mistakes, Sara – as the blind man said to the deaf lady!'

'What?' Sara was really getting her dander up.

Gordon lifted both his hands in defence of his last words. 'Apologies. Not a time for a joke. Like Cal, unfortunately us men do put a size ten in it from time to time.'

'You're not kidding there, buster!' Sara snorted. 'So are you going to do the hocus on me again so I can have this out with grandma?'

'It's not the time, and you are definitely not in the right state of mind for such sensitivities. Always remember that, Sara. Sensitives. They are the ones you go to for clairvoyance. You were put into a state of extreme sensitivity just then in order for you to be able to communicate with the other side. This is why Cal is ahead of you at the moment. Not a criticism, just an observation. Your volatility and mood swings play havoc with such intended contact. Think about it. When you are calm and serene, grandma will come to you again.'

'Is that the end of the lecture?' Sara retorted.

'Well, I suppose so. I can see I must tread warily on your land – even if I have permission, eh, Calvin?' Gordon chuckled, winking at him.

Cal smirked, then caught the look on Sara's face. Storm clouds brewing! He looked down at his feet. 'So now it's a conspiracy? What is all this about, Cal? What land of mine?'

Cal looked at Don Gordon for a next line but he was already heading out through the door, still chuckling. He looked back at Sara, who was tapping her foot, waiting.

'Jesus, Sara, it's not what you think!'

She spat back. 'How do *you* know what I am thinking? It had better be a bloody good explanation or you are for the high jump. Or maybe a black eye, seeing I am so out of practice and lagging so far behind you!'

He sat down in his chair, slumping forward on to the table. Damn it, doesn't she ever take a day off from this trip of hers?

'Can't hide in there, Cal.'

He looked back up at her. She was smirking at him. The relief flooded over him.

'That's better, you two.' Gordon was back in the room with their belongings, including the shards. 'You could be the perfect match. But you need to borrow from each other if that is at all possible.'

'Borrow from each other?' Cal was asking.

'Yes, what's he got that would be of any use to me?' Sara chipped in.

'Mmm! You want the full list or will main points do?' Gordon was chuckling again.

'Full list! You mean I would have to end up as cumbersome, awkward and shy as him?' As she spat this out, Cal winced.

Don Gordon was still chuckling, then stopped. 'Okay, here's my serious face.' He put on a stern expression, but the eyes were still giving him away. They showed he was really enjoying their discomfort. 'Not talking about a complete transplant! Only on the sensitivity side. You're both oversensitive, but Calvin, your shyness turns this into a positive for you as far as the other side are concerned. You can be reached – can be counted on to react favourably when asked. But you need some of Sara's speed of thought and action too, in her own words, "keep up with her!"'

Sara's turn to wince. 'How did you know that?'

'Shards told me. And a bit more. But anyway, Cal, you need to find a bit of Sara's "attitude". Confidence. Sara oozes it but wastes it all by her own oversensitivity.' He paused. 'Now Sara, before you blow up again, let me finish, okay?'

She was tapping her foot again, and looking sideways at the wall.

'I'll take that silence as an okay,' said Gordon, still waiting for an outburst. Sara said nothing. 'Good, very good. Very impressed.'

This did trigger a response. 'Don't do the patronising trick. I will never be comfortable with fucking patronising. And, sorry to interrupt and all that – sir!'

'Very good, Sara. Sorry – mighty average, Sara.' He looked across at her. 'Is that more satisfactory? Not too much praise?'

Sara nodded. She knew instinctively Don Gordon was now well and truly on her case. Whether it was still a professional view and not personal was another matter entirely.

'Not much I can do with you, gal. Better I leave it at that.'

This was definitely *not* what she was contemplating. 'What do you mean?' she asked.

'Sleep on everything that has been said, Sara. I need more time to assess you.'

Sara glared back at him. She was thinking that this was just the line that fucking creep of an analyst had proffered before seducing her. Last time she would ever use a shrink. Still could taste his bad breath!

Gordon could see he had stretched her to the limit so he chose Cal as the way out. 'Calvin – you both now have your possessions back. You are, as far as the authorities are concerned, innocent and free to go. Of course, we know it will only be a matter of time before those who are after you try again. Just be aware. I am on their case too. Not just because the shards deserted you. Michael was dear to me, and that has a tremendous bearing too. But there is something else about this whole business which is drawing me in. It's not easy to confuse or fool me. But again I have been fooled in the past. I need to stay vigilant. I have a strong feeling Djumbola will have to be resurrected in the near future.'

'But where do we go?' Cal asked. Sara was also interested in this reply.

'You both have homes to go to now. They might be a little messed up when you arrive. But bill me personally, and I will make sure damages are met in full. Those morons will pay, one way or another.'

'Are we safe there though?' Cal said.

'Are we safe anywhere, for fuck's sake, Cal?' Sara was retreating out of the door as she spoke only to be halted by the sight in front of her: the two motionless figures of George and Margaret. She froze on the spot. It was as eerie an experience as she could have imagined, especially the woman. Sara had some evil thoughts in her head about what to do next!

But as if reading her thoughts, Cal followed her out of the door and said, 'No way! Remember what you said to me when I was patting that other creep statue. I know you two didn't get on, but I don't think it would be a good idea.'

Sara ignored him completely. She reached under Margaret's skirt, dragging off her knickers. Cal was agog. He heard the sound of guffawing behind him, and realised it must be Don Gordon enjoying the action, but he himself was feeling quite sick!

'It's okay, Calvin. They can't wake up until I tell them to.'

Still chuckling loudly, Gordon went round Cal and proceeded down the stairway, ushering the pair of them to follow. He formally signed them out of custody and then called loudly, 'Hey, George, and you, Margaret. Please cease immediately whatever it is that is causing you both not to be here to sign these folks out of custody.'

The noise alerted a few others in the station. All eyes were on the stairway.

Hoots of laughter followed as the pair descended. Margaret felt a slight breeze on her backside and George was thinking his dead hamster felt a little tighter than usual. But they were both still in a very dazed condition, seemingly having been woken out of a very deep sleep. George was wearing Margaret's underwear, which had been tied tightly around the top of his head.

'Jesus! That's another way of describing getting your knickers in a twist!' some wag from the crowd uttered. Everyone was in stitches.

Gordon turned to Cal and Sara. 'Better make off while there is this distraction. Those two will be coming around in a matter of seconds.'

They needed no second reminder and left the building. Out on the street, several blocks from the station, they entered a café. Ordering coffee and cake the pair got down to talking about their next move. Sara was distracted for a moment by the stares from the adjoining table. 'What's their problem, Cal? What is so interesting about me?'

Cal didn't really want to answer, as it was clear to him sitting opposite her. She had obviously forgotten. 'Sara, I think it might be the...'

She looked at him questioningly. 'Well? Finish the sentence, Cal.'

'The *bandage*, Sara. I think that's what is drawing their attention.'

Sara was on her feet. Cal didn't know whether to follow her or sit tight. His mind was made up for him when she disappeared into the toilets. She emerged minus bandage and resumed her seat. She looked at the occupants of the other table now and gave one of her best frosty smiles.

'Let's scoff this and go.'

Cal was more than relieved to hear that. He just had visions of a major bust-up, followed by jail for genuine reasons!

'So where now?' Sara did not appear to be in the mood for an 'I don't know' from Cal, so he tried a quick response, as Don Gordon had advised.

'Back to your place and coffee?' Expecting another abusive outburst, Cal received a playful slap on the cheek. Okay, then. Fine by me, he thought to himself. Wonders will never cease!

That was until he viewed the aftermath of the goons' visit to Sara's apartment. Absolute mess. It took three hours to get it back to anything like reasonable. Then at last coffee. Then bed!

Cal was woken by a sound. Couldn't quite make out what it was, but there was a slight glow in the far corner of the room. He was sweating and his head was thumping. 'Must be the shards,' he thought, and lay down; but again the sound, like an owl hooting in the far distance, made him rise up again. He scanned the room. He then left the still slumbering Sara in order to investigate. Without his glasses, this was not a good ploy! Slipping across the room, it was surely a certainty he would end up on the floor. Especially as he was in a strange environment. What tripped him was open to question, but the ensuing crash would have woken up Ole Nick, let alone the peacefully sleeping Sara.

On being awakened, her reaction was predictable. 'Christ! What the hell are you doing? Typical man! About to become a father for the first time, and now trying to sneak off.'

Cal was in no mood for this. The fall hurt not just his bones, but on this occasion his new-found pride! 'Quiet, woman. The glow over you. What are you lying on?'

He didn't wait for her reaction, but padded over to where his glasses lay. With normal sight restored he could see that the glow was just beyond Sara, and was now getting brighter. As Cal got closer, the glow intensified and expanded. Then, from the shadows, the familiar cloaked figure emerged. It remained stationary. Neither Cal nor Sara dared move or even breathe, still conscious of what Don Gordon had said about his line being compromised. Could they trust this figure anymore? They had discussed it before going to sleep. Now the question was going to be answered, whether they were ready for it or not. An air of suspense hung round them. But there was something about this apparition which didn't fit the usual cast.

Chapter Seven

The figure stood before them both. Then it proceeded to lift its arms high in the air. The sleeves rolled down, revealing slender arms. But the main features lay on its outstretched fingers: many rings, but one caught their eye immediately. Cal and Sara looked at each other, nodding without speech and acknowledging the identification of a particular ring. The quartz special they had purchased from the old guy's shop! It suddenly glowed as if it had recognised them. The shards were now hovering in the air over the figure, adding their power to an intensifying glare – a melding yellowish-green hue.

Cal had the full force of the join-up, but felt absolutely fine. It was very soothing.

Sara had a similar experience. Initially she didn't like the feeling. She tried to shake it off. But this only caused a further reaction, covering her whole upper body. Squirming at first, she slowly accepted its caress.

An extreme calmness surrounded them both. The figure remained still, allowing the pair to ponder even further the wonder of the ring so recently in their possession. The air became still; a suffocating stillness. Both of them were now gasping for breath. Then, like a bag bursting, the air was released, and so were they. The calmness returned. With this, a soft voice enveloped them.

The hood fell back as the arms were lowered to the sides, revealing a beautiful woman. A nose stud shone brightly, lighting up her face. She was obviously a black woman, but of light skin colour and delicate features. Her eyes were on them. Although kindness shone out, there was also a steely glare somehow mixed with it. Her bearing had a hint of high nobility. Her mouth remained closed but the sound of her voice continued.

'Greetings to you, Calvin. And to you, Sara. I am *Sahariah*. I thank you for your kind efforts on our behalf up until now. Especially for the return of this ring. It is of great importance to me. I am very pleased to be wearing it again. The history of this ring is long and complicated. As with much of your world with corrupted values, they used this ring against its wishes. The return of it to our line has enormous ramifications. The balance is now achievable. But one thing remains a major problem. You have met *Djumbola – he of the scars...*

'The scars represent his status. He is an absolute. Nature's healer. But yet a terrible bridge for one to cross. Which, unfortunately, some in your world have been successful in reaching. Fools to a man! I would not wish to be them now. You have but glimpsed his pain. He would never allow that to be shared by anyone else, least of all me. I have witnessed it with him, though. His cries to the skies, asking why all stand back when they should react. Why do they always allow the bastards to have their own way?

'He considers that money and money's worth to be the root of it all. Who now amongst us can disagree? And that goes up to the highest echelons. He has often cursed those who would covet such wealth to the prejudice of liberty for the rest of humanity and nature. But this sickness over wealth has blinded most of your peoples to such an extent that it seems all are now chasing an impossibility. The balance has been severely affected. The rest of nature cries out for assistance. Whole species on the brink of extinction. Djumbola hears those cries and is bound to react. After all, Djumbola is nature's *own son*.

'The barrier for us is his hatred. That scorn he has deep in his soul for all the bad he has witnessed. Believe me, he has regained the power to obliterate all. And I, for one, could not blame him for this. I did not always feel this way and have personally intervened in the past; appealing to the magic for his powers to be diminished, even taken away entirely. I regret some of this now. It just made for worse experiences for him to suffer. We have witnessed the betrayals, the beatings, tortures and other unspeakable practices of that vile line who have their grip on your world. All they can excuse it with is to declare their actions are for the good of all and for liberty – their form of liberty. That means freedom for themselves and slavery for the rest. Liberty without freedom!

'Djumbola had such a soft merciful nature before *they* came. It changed him into a terrifying sight, unrecognisable to us. We thought by diminishing his power it would assist him to find his way back. But we could never have been so wrong. It just made him worse. He copied their terrible ways at times, showing no mercy. A terrible sight in battle. He, the ultimate warrior chieftain. So many bloody battles…

'We now admit our mistakes and wish to make reparation to him. But it is difficult as he appears to be ignoring us. This is why we have enlisted your kind assistance. Your help is invaluable to our efforts in preventing Djumbola carrying out this threat. We simply wish him to lift his curse and let nature take its course.

'He has been silent for a long time. You have words from him now which he would never convey directly to us. He trusts you. And that is a feat in itself, believe me! He has been watching over you throughout. We know this. His protective powers in your world exceed our own. You will be aware of our own problems, and we are eternally sorry for the injury caused you. We are still tracing the fault, but I have no doubt Djumbola will find it first. Whoever is responsible will be quaking now, for I sense Djumbola is near to his quarry!

'I must, regretfully, take my leave of you. My time is up. I apologise for not letting you ask questions, but I had little time in which to explain. Believe me, those who have previously come in my place were horrified by my insistence in visiting you unaccompanied. But I considered it my duty, in the circumstances – and mine alone.

'Please pass on to Djumbola my regards. His son also misses him. Good fortune to you both.'

Tears were now steaming down Sahariah's face as she stepped back. 'Forgive me.'

Her head was lowered and she was gone.

Both Cal and Sara sat in stunned silence. Another bout of celestial misgivings; the plot was thickening all the time. But this was not your average Agatha C mystery.

'Wow! What now, Sara?' Cal said, coming out of his stupor.

Sara was back to her own best. 'Beats me, honey. Maybe we have some matchmaking to do. But not with anything like the normal relationship problems.' She winked at him.

Cal looked a little shaken by her response. 'How can you be so upbeat about it?'

'There is something else. I sense it. Call it woman's intuition. She isn't just sad because of her split with the black guy. I think there is something else equally important to her. I just have this feeling – a very strong feeling – that she was about to tell us more... ask us to help with something else. Whatever it was didn't rate as highly as reining in Djumbola. Not in her eyes, anyway. But probably the rest of them back there where she comes from didn't rate it as that much of a problem. That is why she came alone.' Sara looked at Cal. 'Only one other thing can affect a woman like that. Remember when the goldfish bowl came the second time. The images of a woman and child – her child. It's to do with her son. I strongly feel that. Maybe he is in danger.'

Cal looked stunned. 'So maybe he has come looking for his father?'

'No maybe about it, Cal. Something is telling me a big *yes* on that!'

Chapter Eight

Djumbola had been born in this life in a remote village in Central Africa. Adopted soon after by a missionary couple hailing from Scotland, he had been christened Donald *Gordon*.

His parents were kindly folk. Initially they had been concerned over his facial scars, not really believing the version given by the village midwife that they had been there at birth. They tended to believe there was some other ulterior motive, but did not press this claim in case there was a change of mind. Marie, his adoptive mother, doted on him – perhaps a little too much! He was a spoilt wee monkey! Donald never took offence over this, even when he realised later the monkey and black connection. Term of endearment from mother to son. His father, Jack, however, was not so forthcoming, perhaps being a little jealous. Donald always wondered if he might also be a little prejudiced as well. Ironic, considering his profession!

They had travelled extensively, so Donald was given a highly varied upbringing. Many different cultures contributed to his prominence as a highly educated young man. But the ethics of his adoptive parents' Christian zeal were lost on him, much to their disappointment.

When they eventually returned to Scotland in retirement, his Uncle Douglas, a prominent Freemason, took him under his wing very early on; so Donald's future was assured. He quickly rose through the ranks, and was highly respected and efficient in his roles as an Advisory Consultant to the International Security Services.

He was not without enemies, though. As if moving up so fast within the ranking structure would not have been cause enough for such jealousy in its own right; being the wrong colour lit a flame of extreme prejudice. But he knew why he had to hold *this* ground.

Don Gordon, on returning from the police station which had earlier witnessed the scenes involving Cal, Sara, George and

Margaret, entered a building which secretly housed offices containing such classified information that only top ranking security were allowed access on to certain floors.

He entered unannounced. George *Coney*, of the tight wig and underwear, was busy in his office poring over a file. He hadn't noticed Gordon's arrival. Gordon shrunk back over to the other side of the room, which also housed the typing pool. Fortunately, it being that late in the day, all but one of the typists had left. The only one remaining was too busy finishing off her work to be bothered with the man now crouching beside her desk. Even when she had completed her task, the typist completely blanked Gordon's apology for bothering her, making her way out of the room without a glance back, front or sideways. Eyes down, heading for the weekend break!

Coney finished with his reading, grabbed up the file and put it under his arm. He began to exit the office but then appeared to have a change of mind. Turning, he approached a large bureau which he opened and locked with the file inside.

Gordon now was curious. He stood up straight and made his way past Coney's office as if he had just arrived. Coney suddenly noticed him and froze. Gordon made out he had not seen him and entered another office further down the hall. He sat down at the desk, and out of the corner of his eye watched Coney's next movements.

Coney appeared extremely uncomfortable. First he went back to the bureau, unlocking it; then he appeared to have second thoughts and locked it again.

George, dear old George! If you are black and afraid of 'whitey', this is your man. Definitely 'pointy hat' time. Another member of the funny grip club. But at lower levels than Gordon. And didn't he just hate that! Did it not stand out a mile to anyone who was looking hard enough. Trouble being there wasn't anyone else. Only Donald Gordon noticing.

And on top of it all, Don had just embarrassed the son of a bitch beyond anyone else's comprehension. This George Coney was the ultimate back-slapping, loud and safe in his own congregational gathering, high-aspiring Masonic dickhead. He wanted to make it to the top and was prepared to cut corners to achieve this goal. Don had thought of the many idiot top men he had met in his time. George Coney *would* unfortunately make it. He was definitely on course – save for one problem. He had to get past Donald Gordon first!

Coney had the right kind of connections, but many of them were of the same ilk, only out for themselves and thus easily put off from seconding someone who could upset their own apple cart. Don had made it his business to spread the word about George. Secretly, no one would now touch him with a barge pole.

No, he would forever be doing the menial tasks. Like interviewing suspects on the strange sects. But with strict instructions. However, not even that could this sorry piece of Kentucky shit manage to do.

Michael Stein. Don had known him for so long. A brother. White, but of the same cause. Took risks, which warmed Don Gordon's soul, although he worried for him. No more worries for Michael. Don sniffed back more silent tears, looking over at Coney with a renewed hatred. He got up and helped himself to a cup of coffee from the office machine. He was still not making any overt sign that he'd noticed Coney, who now was on the telephone conducting an animated conversation with whoever, his back to Don.

Suddenly, Coney swivelled around to face Gordon. But Don's back was to him as he drank his coffee. Terminating the call, Coney got up from his desk. Donning his jacket, he sped out of his office without looking back. Gordon had a mirror strapped to his foot poking out beyond the desk.

'Someone is going to catch up with you, Georgie boy!' Don was now tapping his pen against the desk top.

He then thought of his sidekick. George always seemed to be paired up with her: Margaret *Madison*, aka 'Maddie the mad cow'. Nicknamed thus for obvious reasons apart from among her superiors, who appeared to revere her – especially George. Don didn't want to think too much about how close the two were. Maybe she shaved and he wore it tight. Just don't let them breed! Don chuckled at the thought. But he soon came back out of that levity remembering they were instrumental in Michael's death. But who gave the order?

Gordon sat it out while the floor was emptying. He was on his fifth cup of coffee, but this was all par for the course. He made out he was studying case reports lying handily on the desk he had chosen. In his capacity as a senior security advisor with top level classification clearance, nothing would appear suspicious about his being there. But one thing was obvious to him: nothing had seeped through to this end concerning the toupee'd wonderboy. Given the nature of people in the light of what had been an hilarious prank, a quick call to all stations would have caught on like lighter fuel on a nigger bonfire. But not this time. Don was wondering, maybe this son of a bitch has more connections than I had appreciated. If so, where am I?

He didn't wait for an answer. Don was pretty pissed off now. He tried Coney's office door. He had left in such a hurry. Unlocked. Like your fucking brain, George, you slack-assed fucker! Gordon went straight to the bureau, sizing it up. His hand rested on the left side of it. He co-ordinated a thump with a wrench of his right hand. He was in. He stood back and looked for signs of forced entry. None. Still had the knack. Felt good. He reached in for the file but something else took his eye. Don looked back around him. Was he still alone, or was this some kind of perverted game show, where some fucker was about to spring out and surprise him with stories concerning Auntie Louise?

In the bottom of Coney's drawer was a small pool of dried blood. On top of this lay a plastic bag containing a hairpiece. Don picked it up. Opening the bag, he reached in. It felt damp. He dropped it as soon as he realised. 'What the fuck!' Gordon exclaimed. He rooted around and found what he considered was the file that Coney had been so interested in. Beside it was another bizarre publication. He picked this up instead.

Wigs and Wigwhammys was the title. It was a good job he had had the presence of mind to sit down before opening this magazine. Don sat there for longer than he really should have felt safe with, given the circumstances... but such was the content! As he turned the pages the images were graphical and – to Don – very, very personal. 'Jesus. Where are you? Look at what these fuckers can still do in this day and age!'

The magazine was offering genuine Native American scalps:

'Old or new.' 'Dollars make the difference!' It also contained buying and selling advertisements, all under a general box number – which of course meant everything had to go through the magazine's own checking system. And, Don thought, this must amount to some kind of strict security. If Coney, who else amongst the general cross-section of perverts? He had already reckoned paedophile activity, along with drug barons and their runners, was already being soundly protected and with cover-ups galore – the former because so many of the fuckers were on the list, and the latter because huge amounts of money were involved. He knew this, but to say anything would bring in the whistle-blowing police – the inquisition he had met before. To him it was the same smell.

Don Gordon was now even more pissed than anyone should have made him! He sat awhile, then remembered at last why he was in the office. He stood up again, but felt a little unsteady on his feet and sat down. The scalping mag had got to him. This belonged to someone who should be protecting the public. How many other secret organisations like this were being covered up by the main body of impenetrable secrecy?

He sucked in breath, reached in amongst the files and found again the one Coney had just deposited. Not hard to discover as it shouted out at Don: *Red Code Five*. Highest classification. But not unusual for it to be pulled for this department, the floor being classified for such. But it also had 'NOT TO BE REMOVED FROM THE CHAMBER' stamped across it.

Don sat a while longer at Coney's desk just looking at the cover before opening the file, and gathering his senses. He was still wondering if this all was a trap. He was still mighty suspicious. His senses were not giving him a better conclusion. He opened the file. As he read through, names sprang up at him. So did a lot of information which could have only come from one source: *His line*.

> Michael STEIN. Terminated on instructions from XCHIANG'S Office. Calvin TULLEY and Sara ALONSO: to be terminated. Instructions from XCHIANG'S office. Donald GORDON: termination order suspended. Instructions from Origins Unknown at present.

Don took the file out of the office and headed up the stairs to the next floor. He knew a safe computer there which would not set off any alarms. Programming in the code number from the file, he waited, now in suspense – a level he hadn't experienced for a while. But he could sense that the suspense could be heading through the roof!

The computer fizzed back a reply. <Code number successful. Code word?>

'Jesus. Now I have a problem. Man, is this a white man's paradise or not?' Don punched in a word grasped from his knowledge of how these words are assimilated.

<Sorry, this word is not recognised.> Pause.

<Try again.>

'Fuck you, lady! Wherever did you get that smooth fucking reply from? Shove it where the moon don't shine!' Don knew this conversation wasn't going to last into a relationship.

Don keyed in another favourite. Again, a negative response. He sat forward in the chair. His reflection shone back from the screen. He looked. Then looked deeper. 'Shit and brains don't usually go together. But I am a corned-up kind of slave guy. But how am I gonna spell it. Last chance, you sad fucking African.

He entered 'RUNAWAY'.

<Thank you, sir. Access achieved. You can now search our system.>

'One fucking "N"! Two fucking "N"s an' this black boy waz dun fo'!'

Don Gordon wasted no more time. He read quickly through all updates. One situation spat out another problem at him. But he would take care of that later. His senses were still expecting an attack. Where were they? Another couple of minutes and they would be too late!

Gordon knew what he had to do. He keyed in the word 'ABORT'. He was asked the usual questions on whether he was sure he wished the system to abort. Then he was asked for the code word for system cleansing. Again he sat there, flummoxed. What now? Then, in an another inspirational moment, he keyed in the word 'GNAIHCXGNAIH', before instructing the wiping of memory of the whole system. Don also changed code number and word accesses. He had bought time. He needed time. *Nefaurau* was here. They *knew* he was here.

Nefaurau. Son of Sahariah and Djumbola.

Don Gordon sat in a chair looking through a window over the scene below. The streets were now deserted but he sensed a lurking somewhere out there, convinced now that it was a set-up, a trap. They were now waiting for his next move. Except that Coney had provided him with an unexpected card, and he was now going to trump them. On top of this he was going to deal a severe blow to George and his cronies. Big time! Don knew all too well that to present the magazine in official circles would mean a very in-depth enquiry, followed by a judicial review. And in the meantime, some fuckers were being well paid out of a situation where not just those who were guilty of so much, but also those who perpetrated and encouraged the situation, were going to get off thanks to some clever legal eagle. Some fucking fair system to be proud of!

Don had popped the offending magazine into an envelope and then into the internal post tray. He had a contact on the Indian Affairs Committee, JD White Crow, who thankfully was also a Special Investigator, cleared for this classification level. Don had added his personal card with the very briefest of details on the back. But JD would understand why Don had targeted him with this information. Especially as Don had promised him on some drunken special agents' night he would give him any leads tracing those fuckers' activities amongst his people.

He'd licked the envelope and sealed it and only then realised he hadn't wished JD good luck, but he would know that anyway; JD had said so himself. Don was always good luck for him. They had completed the ceremony. Blood on blood. Both proud!

He cut the lights on the whole floor. Don could now see clearly outside, but anyone out there looking back would now be hampered by the darkness above them. There were no facing buildings of similar height, a precautionary measure for the security of that building which now worked in Gordon's favour. He was aware that they might have night sights, but according to the files he wasn't yet a target for assassination. Yet that could change at anytime, he thought – especially if they got wind of his latest actions!

Then he noticed the movement. Figures scurrying towards the building. He watched their progress closely, timing his own move. As the first body of men entered the ground floor, Gordon took to the stairs, going upwards. Reaching the top floor, he barged through the emergency exit, gaining access to the roof.

Once on the roof he began to remove his clothing. Then he sat down on the cold, gravelly floor space and began chanting quietly. He hadn't used this one for a while. He hoped it would work!

The first of the intruders reached the roof. At the same time a helicopter clattered in, pouring light over the area. All that was visible and could be found was a neatly folded pile of clothes!

Cal and Sara were sitting down at the table enjoying their evening meal. The shards gave the first indication of an arrival. They glowed ever brighter, until, in a brilliant yellow light, the naked figure of Donald Gordon, aka *Djumbola*, appeared. They both gasped, spilling food back onto their plates.

He spoke to them. 'My two young friends, I would be most honoured for you to accompany me back to my humble dwelling. We have much to discuss. On the other hand, you had better come with me pronto because that rabble are on to you and have cessation warrants for you both.'

Cal asked in his bewilderment. '*Cessation warrants?*'

'Like you do when answering the door as good citizens trusting these fuckers. And *ping* – you're dead. And in the report, who fired first? And I know you would say, "We weren't armed." But let's face it, if someone comes up to you showing a valid ID from the many government departments or police offices, you would trust it, wouldn't you? This is an eternal argument. You let them in. Me? I would have already had my gun out and shot the fuckers there and then, no question about it.'

Sara now became animated. 'What do you mean? And forgive me for bringing this up, but your Hush Puppies are missing.' At this, Cal looked confused.

'It is alright, Calvin. What Sara is trying to convey to you is that I am in a state of undress, which she is feeling uncomfortable with. Is that not so Sara?'

She was for once without an answer. Cal was becoming even

more confused, and Djumbola spoke with urgency. 'There is no more time. Please close your eyes tight. No peeking. Empty your mind of all thoughts. If this does not work we will all be left out there somewhere. I don't want that, and I am certain neither of you do either.'

Cal and Sara complied as best they could but Djumbola knew he had overplayed the situation. His power would be sufficient but he wanted them to believe it really crucial. And their immediate compliance was vital. There was a flash, which also registered in the eyes of those who had just broken down the door into Sara's apartment. The pair of them actually sneaked a squinted glance and witnessed them. The eyes of the intruders, as wide as saucers, were still in their minds as they landed in Djumbola's camp.

There was another mighty flash, which penetrated Cal's and Sara's senses.

'You can open your eyes now.'

As they did so, both gasped.

Don Gordon had now completely transformed himself. Djumbola was now sitting cross-legged on a stone floor covered with straw, still naked. His painted face was reflected in the firelight and shadow. The fire in the centre of the room sent flames coursing up to the ceiling. The stars shone outside of this in the beyond.

Dark rings of blue surrounded his already blackened eyes. Red and yellow streaks ran across his scarred cheeks. But crawling all over him were all manner of wildlife!

Cal spied a scorpion, tail up, on his chest. Alerted by Cal's stare, Djumbola looked down and spat on the scorpion. The tail arched further but in that split second he flicked it with his tongue across at Sara. She squealed as it struck her chest, moving rapidly backwards at the same time trying to get out of its flight path; but it stuck to her chest. Cal went to brush the scorpion off but then thought better of it. It wasn't moving. But Sara wasn't aware. Her eyes were now tight shut, her chin elevated upwards from her breasts.

'It's not moving, Sara.' Cal was now looking closer. 'No. It's not alive now – by the looks of it, anyway.'

Through gritted teeth and still not looking down Sara hissed at Cal. 'Get it *off* me, you moron! Off me. Get it *off*!'

Cal again looked closer and thought it had taken the form of some kind of toy badge. He tried to brush it off, but as soon as his fingers touched it the scorpion began to move. Cal jumped back.

Sara, her eyes still closed tight, asked, 'Has it gone, Cal? *Cal?*'

Before he could reply, Sara opened her eyes and screamed. This triggered Cal into action. Summoning up courage, he thrust out his hand, flicking the creature off Sara. As it dropped to the floor it made a pinging sound: back to being a toy badge. Cal was now really confused. He picked it up cautiously and put it in the palm of his hand. He peered at it, his nose nearly touching its back. The scorpion began to move again, tail arching to the extreme... Cal's turn to scream! He dropped it on the floor and the scorpion scuttled back to Djumbola's seated position. Climbing his leg, it settled, nestling in his crotch. This area of his body was teeming with wildlife, including all manner of creatures: ants, moths, butterflies, spiders, flies, beetles and such; all fighting for space in a heaving mass hiding his entire manhood.

'Not all is ever as it seems.' Djumbola was enjoying himself.

Sara let out a wail. 'Where have you brought us? What hell is this?'

Djumbola spoke quietly, as if not to disturb his flock. 'No hell here, Sara. This is just your everyday piece of normality. This is what nature intended – us all getting on with each other.' He chuckled. 'Until it comes to mealtimes, that is!' Again he chuckled dryly. 'Now perhaps I am guilty of getting too close and attached to these specimens, but these are all I have had for company in the many years of incarceration at the hands of enemies. Without them to talk to, I would surely have gone completely mad. But you, Sara, would say I have already reached that state, and beyond, eh?'

Sara was still trying to wipe the invisible stain from her chest, feeling very cutesy. She either did not hear Djumbola or chose to ignore him, not being pleased at what had just taken place.

Djumbola continued. 'I prefer to trust these little ones with my thoughts. After all they are hardly going to spill the beans to the Inquisition, much as that lot would wish to make them talk.

Compared to human beings, at least you can trust that in their nature they will always act as decreed. Nature has made each an individual species. They do not pretend to be anything but themselves. Those that bite. Those that sting. Those that sing—' further chuckling —'and they sense this in me too. They'll only be unfriendly to me if I upset them. How does that compare with human behaviour?'

Cal spoke. 'But you spat on the scorpion, and it didn't like that. Or being thrown around. Nearly stung us.' He looked over at Sara, who was still obviously in shock, continuing to wipe her front.

She shook her head back at him. 'I can't think yet. Still got the feeling of that fucking scorpion. *Yuuukkk!*'

'She would have stung you if I had let her. Then we would have been missing you already. How I hate that line! She is very obedient, don't you think?'

Sara at last came out of her trance. 'You mean you can communicate with her – that fucking thing, creature, whatever? You married to her? Copulate with her?' She was bristling now with fury, especially sensitive to the 'obedience' jibe.

'I must apologise, Sara. And to you, Cal. Perhaps my idea of a little fun is a bit over the top. The scorpion enjoyed the joke too. But again I would think neither of you shared it.' Djumbola was waiting for the next outburst. He put his head down, taking up a handful of the insects which crawled over his hand and upper arms.

'Over the top. *Over the fucking top*! Frightened the shit out of me! Absolutely *not* what I would class as a party trick. I am very, very pissed at you.' Sara glared at Djumbola.

He looked up again and held her stare. 'Point taken. Now to business.'

Sara was not expecting that as an answer. 'What do you mean, business? What kind of business could we possibly have with a naked Blackman going back to nature?' She snorted.

'Then it appears I will have to prompt you. I don't need to, but you are my guests; under my protection, even from scorpions.' He waited for Sara's reaction, which was a further snort, before continuing. 'My line are desperate for my change of mind. They wish me to relinquish my curse on all humanity. But why should I give up what I have had to endure so much for? And my friends? What would be their fate? Why should I release my grip? Because this is what is being asked of me in order to open a door to the bridge. For the evacuation of certain souls back to the other side. But what if they get this wrong? They're hardly giving me confidence in their strategy, seeing the diabolical mess they left you in.'

Cal and Sara were taking this in, both now looking a touch perplexed. 'And what about the rest of nature? Has it not suffered enough already? Human beings and their egos – believing they are masters of nature just because it appears dumb! Far from it, my friends. A very long time ago would be a shock to each and every member of the modern human race!'

'So what are you saying? That everything can really talk? Even the grass and trees... the clouds? I must admit to smoking some shit in the past and getting very weird scenes in my head. But this is so far-fetched,' said Sara, still not down from her shock yet. Cal nodded thoughtfully at her.

Djumbola tried a different tack. 'Okay, say there are only two places left on the other side, and they want you two obviously to be selected. But nature has a scorpion and butterfly it wants to be included instead. Who decides? I would not wish to make such a decision.'

'Are you now trying to compare us – two human beings – with a couple of creatures?' Cal asked.

'And what is wrong with that? I mean, Sara is a match for the scorpion. But you, Cal, may be a little short for a butterfly.'

Sara retorted, 'What has size got to with it? And don't you dare put me in the same bracket as that fucking scorpion!'

'I was talking figuratively, Sara. Similar nature. Deadly if roused.' Djumbola chuckled again. 'And I was not talking about short as in size and strength, Calvin. Intellect!'

'Intellect?' Cal said, looking puzzled.

'Sure, Calvin. Why should human beings believe they have this world's only minds? And with all that combined high intellect, what is done with it? Forming egos – many with an ego too far. Together, forming clubs of back-slapping sceptics. There lies the serious problem.' Djumbola looked at them both in turn. 'Do you blame the rest of nature for acting dumb? They still have natural senses. And the good sense not to let on! And you can't buy these back from nature. No sir! So put away that cheque book mister! If nature were to drop its guard, what would occur? Capture. Captivity. Seems we are back talking slavery. But nature will never be enslaved.'

Cal's chin visibly dropped. He shook his head, looking down at his feet as he was wont to do. From this stance he said quietly, 'People do talk to trees. Talk to birds. Other animals. Horses and the like. Dogs, cats. Some would have these people locked up and the key thrown away. I suppose it also includes me. I even started talking to that rock before I realised how special it was.' He looked up, searching for an answer. Djumbola did not disappoint.

'Who is right and who is wrong? Calvin. That is what you are asking, yes?' Cal nodded, his eyes now on Djumbola's.

'Nature will always listen to the right one. Trust is an invisible sense. Do you understand that, Calvin?' Cal again nodded, warming to this discussion.

'Nature is there to listen to each and every one of us, high or low. Good or bad. Presidents or crocodiles.' He laughed and continued. 'Forgive me I just have to make a little light of some things which sprang to mind. And that comparison!' He again had a chuckle to himself. 'Anyway, these pious types go into their churches and the like, praying for forgiveness and whatever. Who do they think they are talking to? Would it matter awfully to them if it were pointed out? That *it* is listening to you, but what are you offering in return? I mean, take these examples, for instance. The farmer has just taken a subsidy which means, eventually, the culling of his flock. Did nature sanction this? No. Money decided. On the way to the church his 4x4 vehicle strikes and kills another member of our community. Say, a fox. Vermin to humans. But to nature? So the fox lays by the roadside, eventually becoming several meals for carrion crows and the like. And when he arrives at the church he joins the congregation standing alongside bankers, accountants, businessmen – all with the aim of praising a situation. *All things bright and beautiful*. A few less, thanks to the farmer's efforts! But if that farmer had had the misfortune to collide with another human being, would this body have been left lying in the road for the same meat eaters to consume? Of course not. Because human life is sacred. Did nature sanctify that assumption? What nature has had to contend with in human development is a trial in itself. But without doubt, the main concern is the dumbing down of the masses, content with popcorn, hamburgers, easy listening, easy viewing, easy life. No questions, please. Unless it's to do with being an instant millionaire, or on any topic concerning the main fare in popular magazines and the usual round of television soap operas. My apologies. I appear to have gone on a little bit!'

'You can say that again,' Sara retorted. 'You started losing me half a book back! But from what I think you are saying – and you do seem to go around a few houses before finding the right door – that praying, basically, is a waste of fucking time. But I could have saved your breath there and told you the same thing anyway.' Sara ignored Cal's impassioned pleas to stop.

'It is alright, Calvin. Sara has a right to voice her view, however wrong it may be.' Djumbola looked down at the mass still having a delightful time in his nether regions.

Sara was bristling again, looking ready to continue the debate on her own terms. 'Don't you patronise me! You are not that powerful to stop me coming over and giving you a pasting.'

Cal was now so concerned he went to prevent her doing something they would both regret, only to be stopped in his tracks by her wistful smile and words. 'It's okay, Cal. I am only joking. But I do wish I could put that scorpion up Don's darker passage!' Cal winced.

'Calvin, this woman of yours would be an ideal latter-day candidate for Bernard Gouie's school of learning!' Djumbola waited for the response.

'Bernard *who*? Why should I want to be in his school?'

'He was *the* Inquisitor. But even he did not see reason for my burning at the stake in France, which, if you may kindly recall, was followed with my curse on a King and a Pope.'

'So where are we going with this now?' Sara said, still holding her ground.

'Okay. By human contact with each other, that trust is formed over a length of time. Why is this? Because humans have lost that natural sense. It has been stolen from you. That is why so many go wrong and head into disastrous relationships. But you have watched nature programmes on television, have you not? Not many divorcing couples there, huh? No, the senses are still natural. A mate waits for an ideal partner, knowing instinctively, through natural sense, what to trust and what not to. If they get it wrong it's mealtime for another! But I have to say, Calvin, you personally have nothing to worry about on this score. Talk away! They can see and sense you, as they can each other. Natural senses. And my natural sense tells me I can trust you, Calvin. And, Sara, you might be surprised, you too!'

Cal looked down again, feeling humbled. Sara looked Djumbola in the eye, less humbled. Then she looked down, muttering to herself, but just loud enough for the others to hear, 'Take something for me to trust someone who leaves his wife and son to fend for themselves. And I can't stand fucking scorpions!'

Sara looked over at Cal for support. But, unfortunately, he was still taking in the good words directed at him by Djumbola. Cal winked back at her, then seeing her frosty glare, recoiled. Her words stung! 'I can see whose side you are on, you moron!'

That sting earned a retort. 'We are all on the same side, Sara.'

'Speak for yourself, scorpion shit!'

Cal looked back at her horrified. She was madder with him than he had considered. But a faint glimmer of a smirk appeared on Sara's face. She's teasing me again, he thought. Cal looked back at Djumbola, who was shaking his head.

'I impart words of extreme wisdom and all you two can do is prove a point.'

'Very hard to take it that seriously with you covered in wildlife,' responded Sara. 'But you still haven't answered why you left wife and child in the lurch.'

Cal took up the theme. 'I have to agree with Sara – you do cut a bizarre picture with that all over you.' Cal was feeling less intimidated, but whether it was by Sara or Djumbola, he wasn't quite sure. But nevertheless, he felt a little more relaxed.

Djumbola looked over his seething army. 'Okay, enough entertainment, *chaps*.' Incredibly, all the creatures obediently crawled off and away from him, disappearing into the gloom. At first he mimicked colonial speech. 'Never going to get a part in the Bond movies with that face, boy, or Sidney Poitier would have been looking back in the posters at you from those *Doctor No* and *Diamonds are For Ever* fucking films.' Then reverting back to his usual tone, 'But sorry, you white folks. As much as I damned respect the both of you, I have been asked why my sorry ass ain't there – when it ain't pickin' cotton, that is – not there for ma woman and chiaaalld!'

Sara gave him an old-fashioned look which told him she was not impressed, and Djumbola became more serious. 'Alright, I know I have not been there for them sufficiently. In my pursuance of revenge I have tended to neglect certain duties. But I have a feeling that is about to change. Sahariah was upset over something when she visited you both. She would not have made a personal visit alone if it hadn't been important. She obviously did not trust her advisors sufficiently – and that is a problem in itself.'

Whatever was in Sara's mind about her next question over their meeting with Sahariah was dispelled by the sight of the insect army in retreat. It left Djumbola exposed, literally.

Sara averted her eyes from this particular part of his nakedness, but his manhood had already been the subject of her innerfocus. As she closed her eyes, it was still imprinted on her visual senses. Cal's eyes were also riveted. Suddenly realising this, he quickly looked away. Neither of them were still quite ready, though, still reeling from the after-effects of their enforced travels as another blinding flash heralded another; but not for them. Both were looking over to where Djumbola had sat. He had disappeared.

Sara rose to her feet but began to sway. Cal rushed over and held her up; but she didn't object. 'What is going on here, Cal? I am getting just a little fed up with all this. Feeling very tired – and unwell!'

Before Cal could answer, there was another flash, this time so brilliant it took the breath out of them both. Thus it took a while for them to recover, and when they could finally focus both of them let out gasps.

Chapter Nine

Before them was Djumbola dressed in the clothing of a priest of old. Beside him stood a small boy of around ten years of age, dressed similarly. But the boy's face was clean. Clear of scarring. The resemblance, however, was remarkable. Clearly this was Sahariah's son.

Djumbola addressed the pair, who were still blinking in disbelief. 'Greetings again, Calvin and Sara. This is Nefaurau, the son of Sahariah. Unfortunately, he is related to me somewhat. I appear to be this wretch's father.' The boy, glaring, looked up at his father.

Djumbola nodded to him and continued. 'He is a very foolish boy. He defied wisdom given as instruction to him and the *why* of this. He has upset his mother beyond words. His line is not impressed. But, I suppose, like father, like son!'

'Do not presume to patronise me, Father.' Nefaurau's words were as measured as his stare. Sara stifled a laugh, which did not go down well with Djumbola.

'Oh! So you would mock me in front of our guests. Let me remind you now of the position you are in. To this world you have to be born. Or reborn. I know just a little of this. For you to just wander aimlessly into it in search of who knows what is not how nature works, my son. Unfortunately, you are now outside the natural protection your highness would normally expect. You are at the mercy of all here. And some do not wish you well, believe me. Nature cannot offer its usual safeguards to you. The laws of nature here dictate that you are born, live a life – however long or short – then die. Simple as that.'

'But I *am* here, Father. Nature let me pass through the door. It must have been for a reason.' The boy's voice gained another level as he pleaded to be excused.

'Then if it let you in as you say, show me the birth certificate issued to you. Perhaps an entry visa, maybe? Special VIP?'

Nefaurau could see he was not going to better his father's argument. The boy was looking increasingly uncomfortable.

Sara by now was bristling again. Natural womanhood, protecting a brood. 'That's enough. Maybe he's made a mistake. But don't all youngsters? I did. Bet even you did.'

Djumbola nodded in her direction but without taking his eyes off his son. He asked Cal, 'And you, Calvin? Have you anything to add?'

Cal shrugged. 'How bad is it? Is he really in that much danger?'

'Extreme danger. This boy is now at the fate of any who wish him well or not so well. Trouble is, those who wish him well are in the minority in this world. Which leaves a mighty problem. The rest will be after his scent. They know he is here. Now I have already called you foolish, my son. Now I will call you forgetful.'

The boy looked up. 'I am confused over the second accusation.'

Djumbola addressed his next statement with a smile directed at Cal and Sara. 'High-born manners in an infant. They can wear off.' He winked at the pair. Only one smiled in return.

In order to explain, Djumbola squatted down to a similar height to his son. 'A while ago, when I was with you, and I am sorry I have not been there for you enough…'

Nefaurau interjected, 'That is what my mother says continually.'

Djumbola looked to the roof, and then at Cal and Sara. Still only one of them was returning anything like a passable smile! Djumbola's mood visibly began to change. 'My son, you are here for your purpose. I have not the right to interfere; only advise. That is the way of our line, is it not?' Nefaurau looked on his father. He nodded, but with a curious look on his face.

'You remember, however, my always asking of you to remain and protect your mother's interests whilst I was away?'

Nefaurau's face started to darken. The boy knew what was coming next. 'Yes Father, but—'

'No *buts*, Nefaurau. Son of the High Priestess, Sahariah; heir apparent to the line of wisdom; you have failed to honour that agreement. On top of this, you may have left our line exposed by passing through a doorway without properly safeguarding it. It may well be the reason our line has been compromised. And this lady and gentleman received injury to them whilst under the protection of our line, because of that blip. Unforgivable!'

Nefaurau visibly shuddered. His eyes were wide in shock at what had been put to him. He began to stutter a reply but gave up, knowing he was well and truly beaten. And in the wrong. He looked down, and tears began to drip from his cheeks to floor.

Sara said, 'Christ's sake, it was only a scratch. No need for all this upset.' She went to comfort the child but Nefaurau stepped back from her intended embrace. Even though extremely upset, the boy managed a cold frosty stare. Djumbola winked at Sara, who snorted her disapproval and returned to stand beside Cal.

'That is the position, my son. I have spoken about it, and now there's no need to go on. In that, Sara is correct. It serves no purpose. Just requires vigilance, a bit of repair work. And possibly a large dollop of good fortune! By the way, Sara was only offering maternal support, be it in a surrogate fashion. You would have let your mother hug you.'

Nefaurau looked at Sara. 'Maybe I would and maybe not. But my mother is my mother.' Sara shrugged back at him.

'Talking about protection. There is something I still have not been able to recover from in this cruel world you have sauntered into. I have an army. I have talked to you about this. That difficulty to protect when facing overwhelming odds. I have kept back one incident from the past which still haunts.' Djumbola hesitated. He looked visibly shaken.

A slight crackling from the fire. Minutes passed. All eyes were now on Djumbola. Tears were running down his scarred cheeks. No one dared speak. All three showed degrees of discomfort. Even Nefaurau. He held out a hand to clutch his father's. Djumbola withdrew his. Through his blurred vision seeing his son's reaction of hurt, Djumbola brought it back. Hand in hand felt good for both of them.

Djumbola continued. 'A long time ago, on a ridge, stood an army with a prickly, near-defeated leader. All around was the stink, the stench of death. Ours. The other side were roaring in the distance, regrouping, sensing a final victory. This was a new experience for me. I was not used to such a defeat. Suddenly I was brought out of my stupor. Two trusted generals had ridden up to my position. Both dropped from their horses. First they stood in front of me, blinking, looking just below my eyeline. I followed their gaze down to my body. I was covered in butterflies. A fantastic colour scene. In other circumstances it would have been reverence personified. Then in the blink of an eye they were gone. I looked for my generals. They were on their knees, heads touching the ground before me. I bade them rise up. We discussed the ensuing conflict. I said that we should try a final charge. They both assented – but not to my own personal participation. I argued for some time, but they would not be moved. My generals had words of their own above mine. I consequently had to offer deference to their opinions. Subsequently, I watched from that hillside as my army charged those bastards. My army was routed. All died. No one was spared. Because it was *my* army, *my* soldiers, *my* people, I was supposed to be their protector. And here I was sitting on a horse all the way up from them. I turned towards home, no longer caring what happened to me. I drank the liquor. I went without sleep. Finally I awoke in a ditch, freezing. Who woke me? My horse. Yes, he of the faithful breed. And he had words for me. There, Calvin! He said it was my duty to *all* to survive. Nature was calling on me. To remember the flight of butterflies. Nature's sign to me. Everything had a purpose. Even the death of my army. More for me to do. And as it transpired I had victory after victory thereafter. But quietly inside of me I had died in most ways back at that battle scene. Do you understand now, Nefaurau?'

He looked at his father. His answer was a kiss on Djumbola's cheek. Sara looked approvingly at the scene.

Djumbola tried to raise a smile but his mood was still very sombre. 'I still felt remorse, ashamed at what could be construed as cowardice. Still I heard ringing in my ears, the words of those bastards. Taunting me to come down and face them. Which I did eventually, in time. I must admit I spurred my new army on to commit terrible atrocities on them in revenge. But no matter how much blood I spilt I could not recapture the feeling I had before that terrible sight. The magic works in wondrous ways, its wonders to perform. It has been a long painful journey but I am glad now I made it. The discovery of some of nature's more hidden qualities puts everything that occurs into some perspective. But I am certain it contains more. Much more. And it will be passed on to you eventually, my son.'

Nefaurau could not help himself now and flung his arms around his father, who managed a faint smile.

'That's better! I feel so much better,' Sara trilled. Cal looked disbelievingly at her, shaking his head slightly, still feeling in himself a great sorrow at Djumbola's tale. Sara just shrugged.

'It is alright, Calvin. Much of what I have been saying is men talk. Sara is echoing what any woman would truly feel over such a matter. But nothing comes between mother and son. An absolute of nature. She is also happy to see father and son getting on. Sahariah would approve very much of this scene!'

Then he turned again to Nefaurau. 'You will understand now why it is hard for me to contemplate leaving my army unprotected again.'

Nefaurau looked reverently at Djumbola. 'I understand, Father. Mother understands. We all pray for it. But it can never happen. You have built up such a vastness of followers. Your army in total is huge – too many. Please see sense on this. Nature will not allow. Impossible to absorb. You have given a reason why you cannot bear the thought of leaving this behind. But you also say nature has a purpose for everything. It has always found you again when you have cast yourself adrift. It wants to find you again now. Father, I have not made this journey without giving much consideration to *all*.'

It was Djumbola's turn for reverent looks. His son had marshalled a fine argument at such a tender age. He quietly felt proud of his son. 'Well said! Only a close relative could induce a sign like this in me. I am greatly moved, actually shaken by the force of your entreaty. I will, of course, give your words much thought.' Djumbola looked across at Cal and Sara. 'Nefaurau – Calvin and Sara will look after you here while I attend to a little matter. Then I promise I will accompany you home.'

'Wait, wait here!' Sara was now feeling pretty agitated – or pretty in her agitation! 'I am hearing a lot to do with you and your lovely son, but what about us?'

Cal was nodding his agreement to Sara's question.

Nefaurau looked a little confused, listening to the conversation. 'Why are your servants addressing you in this matter, actually questioning your orders?'

Djumbola looked up at the roof, knowing full well what a gaffe his son had committed. 'They are *guests*. My guests, my son.' He was going to explain further but Sara burst into full song!

'Servants? *Servants*? Please explain. The more I am witnessing this the more I do not understand what the hell is going on. Cal, come on, get your coat, we're leaving.'

Sara grabbed Cal's hand and made for the exit. But she stopped suddenly, causing Cal to bump into her in his mild daze. 'Where *is* the exit?' she said, turning back to Djumbola. 'How does one get out of this fucking place?'

Djumbola studied them both for some time, making Cal and Sara feel more uncomfortable by the minute. Djumbola had this way of stretching any given situation to the maximum effect. Sara especially was now regretting her impulsiveness. He eventually sighed and spoke to them in a tone reminiscent of a schoolteacher's admonishment.

'Responsibility is hard for anyone to take. Please forgive my son's ignorance. Of the ways of this world he has yet much to learn. He has been surrounded by a certain level of privilege, ages old. I came through the same academy but never could accept its teachings on class systems. It is even worse here in this world. I keep hearing about the so-called "high born" and "survival of the fittest". The rest of nature adheres to that theory, of course; but in a natural order. Disciplined, orderly. Human beings, without thinking they need the same level of self-discipline have borrowed from nature's system but have perverted and twisted its meaning to suit an unnatural state of affairs. Survival of the *richest*, more like. God-ordained Royalty and clergy. The whole system propped up by the most unnatural of commodities. When I see money growing on trees I will finally have accepted that nature can be bought. Until then, privilege will get a rough ride from the likes of me. Unfortunately, Nefaurau cannot see you yet as equals. He and I are worlds apart in this regard. As far as I am concerned our line of old preferred to measure this privilege in wisdom and social awareness. High born does not mean being there to look down on others, but to use that increased awareness and wisdom for the benefit of *all*. To guide and protect. But this world of yours has been all but completely ruined by the near saturation levels of moral and financial corruption. I have heard it said that everyone eventually has his price. I, like the rest of nature, cannot agree. But while the majority of humanity can be seduced by promises of potential riches, all will have to end with a *bang*! Literally. Remember the asteroid? Or *Djumbolastone* as my kind friends have named it. Appropriate, I think!'

'You mean it is actually going to happen?' asked Cal. 'We keep hearing rumours of it. Then we are told it will be dealt with. Scientists, the military, all having ideas on blowing it up, or deflecting it.' He was in his element again. He just loved talking about things like this; especially if there was a hint of cover-ups.

'Afraid so, Calvin. Nature is not going to wait forever for humanity to change things back. She is self-regulatory. I sense her patience with mankind is exhausted. Thus a big bang! Have to say, not before time either. Look at the greed, arrogance, ignorance and cruelty of people who then pray to a God for forgiveness without meaning a word of it. Absolute hypocrisy everywhere! Placing at the same time massive burdens on the rest of you good and kind people. Add to that the terrible state of nature, and what has been done to it in the name of human progress. Yes, it's time for that to end. But of course, this is the pressure on me to assist my line rather than go my own way. That bridge I spoke of.'

'The *bridge over troubled waters*,' Sara offered.

'Mmmm! Simon and Garfunkel. Good, Sara. And there is another song by Fleetwood Mac about a bridge bringing us back together,' Cal enthused.

'A lot of songs have subliminal content as well. Some of it passing on good vibes. Others not so healthy,' Djumbola stated. 'But that is another situation altogether, as yet to be addressed. However, I am certain Nefaurau will now learn and quickly assimilate another perspective. His limited experience, I think, is being updated even as we speak. He will still treat you both as secondary, according to his upbringing. But I warn you, my son, do not incur any more wrath – especially in the lady!'

'Yes, yes. Have a go at Sara time again. I walk straight into situations because of my short fuse. La-la-la! Can't hear you!' Sara was walking now around the perimeter of the room. 'So where does a lady go to powder her nose? This is a mud hut!'

Djumbola gave an answer equally tongue in cheek. 'A mud hut to you, maybe. But it has been home to many tribes. Many races. Many going back to *the* time. When we had to make sacrifices for *all* to survive. So you ask where you go to make pretty. Where did any of the tribeswomen go? Outside of the tent, or mud hut as you put it. But I warn you now, stray too far out of this hut and you will fall very far. Each is a bubble. Home for those who choose it as a safe haven away from the bad lands. Or for use in encasing the bad lands, if you get my drift. For most there would be no escape. Can you imagine what perceived hell that would be for privileged and corrupt souls from your world!'

Sara began to walk out of the hut and then hesitated, stepping back, cursing. 'I need the loo!' She was looking a little desperate.

Djumbola chuckled at her discomfort. 'Stop cursing, then, and ask out loud.' He watched as she looked back at him, mouthing swear words without sound. Her need was becoming greater.

'Toilet. I need to pee.'

Djumbola decided to do the honours for her. 'The lady is in need of toilet facilities. Please open a doorway!' And duly an opening appeared before her.

She rushed into the light, returning some while later very light-ened! She wore a large smile on her face as she looked across at the magician that was Djumbola.

He merely nodded back at her thank you to him. 'This is not a prison. If you wish you can put yourselves back where you were. All you have to do is speak it. I have authorised it. But with Nefaurau it is more complicated. He can also still leave. However, I would hope he does not after hearing my words. And yourselves too. All that is here is for your hospitality. I am most hospitable to those I care for, but hostility rages in me for those I detest. For those fools who incur my wrath, there is no such freedom of movement. And definitely no exit! You can ask for anything within reason. Some would call this heaven. But it is also so close to what

95

you would class as hell. Make no mistakes. Please.'

Nefaurau spoke. 'Where are you going, Father?'

Djumbola turned to his son, placing a hand on the boy's shoulder. 'I have a little mopping up to do,' he replied; but he could see that this was not going to be a sufficient answer. 'Alright. I will give you a broader explanation.' He sat down beside Nefaurau, who took his lead from this and perched himself on a log. Sara and Cal also made themselves comfortable.

Djumbola looked across at Cal and Sara, addressing his main discourse towards them. Nefaurau understood that this knowledge would possibly be of more consequence to the other two. He acknowledged this without any more movement than a slight nod to his father; they understood each other.

Djumbola began to speak. What Cal and Sara had previously had in mind to ask Djumbola was pretty well covered by his words. Not a lot was left unanswered.

'When I arrived at your flat wearing a lot less than I am now,' he said, and chuckled; but seemingly Nefaurau wasn't getting the joke, 'I had to leave my clothes behind. The spell would only work whilst naked.' He directed this at the boy, who nodded sagely.

'I was being chased off by our mutual acquaintances. They were after me for one reason or another yet to be established. But I am quite certain that they will not yet be aware of the total impact of my last few moments in the building. I discovered a file containing in depth personal information on all of us, including your arrival my son.'

Nefaurau nodded again but the pair were animated. Sara spoke first. 'What sort of information? My God, they can't go around doing things like that! There are laws against such invasion of personal liberty, surely?'

Cal was equally disturbed. 'What can be done about it, Djumbola? This means we will be forever followed, watched, picked up, interrogated... locked up.'

'I must admit to being as shocked as you are now. But I should not have been that surprised; after all, I do work amongst them. But there is more. I managed to read through a fair bit in a very short space of time, snatching at paragraphs here and there. I am deeply indebted to a person least likely to be on my Christmas card list. Remember the George and Margaret show?'

Both nodded, now showing much interest in what Djumbola had to say.

'Well, that idiot George took the file marked "Not to be removed" from a maximum security vault to his office to peruse. Unfortunately for him, I noticed and recovered it from his cabinet after he left. Not only that but I discovered a magazine – no, not pornographic for him. Selling old and, would you believe it, *new* scalps to be used for hairpieces. Even had a live one in there. Sitting in a plastic bag, still damp.'

Sara let out a low moan. 'Jesus, what kind of people are they? What more can they be up to?'

Cal still hadn't fully taken the meaning in. 'What you are saying – there are people still scalping our Indians like they did all those years ago? But how do they get away with that?'

'You would really not want to know, believe me. I believe ordinary citizens want to be reassured that in the event of being threatened by anything as terrifying as that they would be able to find someone to assist them. But I wouldn't hold my breath. That is why the magazine is now in the hands of a reliable contact. And a Native American at that! George and his cohorts won't know what hit them. If you can't find the solution by going to the top, find your own way. But not everyone has those kind of contacts. And I don't think there are many of my friends now who will wish to be entangled in the mesh with me, no matter how much they like me. Even for them, I have probably gone too far this time. But what the hell!'

Nefaurau got to his feet. 'Father, tell me what have you done? I know you always promised a massive attack on their line. Is it done now?'

Djumbola turned now so that he was able to direct an answer to all three. 'What my son is referring to is something I told him a while back: that if I ever had the chance to seriously disrupt their web of intrigue, I would. And have. The file contained code numbers, and I was most fortunate with the choice of code words. I managed to get in, and instructed the system to wipe all memories. Destroyed all back-up functioning procedures to boot.

Their whole web of information and communication will be slowly disintegrating as we speak. And I altered the codes. Hopefully, it will take them quite a while to even get into the system before they realise just how much of an impact one lone Blackman can have on whitey's world!'

Cal whistled in admiration. Sara said, 'So all the information on Cal and myself was destroyed too?'

Djumbola nodded. 'Every single bit of information on everyone they were interested in. All gone!' Sara clapped her hands, letting out a shrill squeal of delight and relief.

'I have my reasons for hating them. Nefaurau knows those reasons well. I detect he has also a deep contempt for them, even in one so young. Anyone from our line who knows the truth about them will feel as we do. Their line is full of corruption. In fact, I would say it is a prerequisite of their order that such corruptibility is endemic in each of their souls. Deviants, perverts, cowards, bullies and hypocrites are all attracted to this evil club, all feeding from the same trough. A line of miscreants from the highest echelons down through the ranks to the lower classes, who can be bought at the drop of a penny to act as faithful foot soldiers, forming protective rings around each layer of the class system. *Their* class system. Formed for the sole purpose of keeping power – not natural power, but that gained through riches. It sickens me to see the bowing and scraping given these liars and cheats who are only on pedestals because of wealth. Not because they are wise and protectors of liberty. Anything but. For they have no collective conscience. And from this no one is accountable. There's no accountability anywhere. They just keep pushing the problem around – unless of course the whistle-blowing police can find a scapegoat. Some poor wretch to feed to the public in their ignorance. The baying mob having been whipped up into a fury by the darker powers of spin-doctoring conducted under their covert instructions. Oh, I know well this clever procedure which has been directed at me in the past on more occasions than it is healthy for me to remember! No. No caring outside of their own tight circles of self-interest. The world economy sitting in their vast wallets. And getting back to what I said earlier: if anyone has a real problem – I mean, a *real problem* –

where to go with it? The true answer in most cases is there is simply no quarter that can be trusted to give a fair hearing. Always there's a brick wall of indifference, especially if it involves anyone from that exclusive "club". But it's worse if you rattle their cage too loudly, upset their cosy protected world, threaten the dominant web they have weaved. Then there is a strong chance of your disappearance... being contracted out. Like *dead*! Ain't no scruples amongst this bunch.'

The contempt in Djumbola's words was unmistakable.

Cal was agog. 'But you have just ruined part of that web you are talking about. Aren't you afraid? Jesus, you will be in their "most wanted" deck of cards!'

'What's to be afraid of? What can they do to me that hasn't been done before? In any case, their power will be crumbling alongside the web. A lot of financial information was in those systems. Whole series of secret bank accounts and investments now rendered inoperative. Take 'em years to untangle the mess. Break the money system and they fall down with it. And that damned rock is heading toward them at the same time. What a headache!'

'But you, Djumbola, you could be – with your power, all the things you can do – the people's champion.' Cal was trying to sound convincing, and Sara actually backed him up.

'Didn't think I would ever say this to you. But at the moment you are some special hero – wiping that information off and causing those bastards so much grief.'

Djumbola smiled at them both. 'Thank you, Calvin. And thank you, Sara. Thank you, but no thank you. With respect, I seem to remember someone trying to save this world. For all his efforts, did he not end up nailed to a cross?'

Cal looked down. Sara looked away.

'Their Christ, Father?' Nefaurau asked. Sara and Cal's heads did an about front!

'Yes, my son. And you know I witnessed the event. I'm still angry over the hypocrisy of the whole religious spectrum. But I will not be drawn any further into that debate. It is for higher powers than me to sort that one out. And you, Sara, talking in terms of heroism... most unlike you!'

'Slip of the tongue. Didn't mean it at all!' She smiled back at him.

'Dangerous to be the wrong kind of hero in this world. Their line don't like a smart ass. That's why *he* ended up on the cross. Perhaps that's why all your heroes only appear as actors on screen or in kids' comics. I mean, how long would any of them last kicking major butt in the real world? And their salaries wouldn't be anything to shout about. So no exposure from the media, which only seem to want to talk with and about *rich* people – to put in the faces of less than rich people. Oh! Here I go again. Let's just agree their ain't no Stallones, Arnies, Clints, or Charles Bronson *Death Wish* types offering up their much needed services to the downtrodden. Never going to happen whilst the money men rule. Now I must take my leave and possibly cause a little more disruption.'

'You will be careful, Father?' Nefaurau was now frowning. For a little boy, even a high-born child, this was an immense amount to take in unexpectedly and in such a short space of time.

'Do not worry on my behalf. I promise you I will take great care to avoid possibility of detection. It's in my interests to keep in the shadows. Can't expect to wreak any more havoc if I am in their sights!'

Nefaurau looked down, and in that moment Djumbola stepped back and disappeared. A small voice followed his departure, calling after him. 'Good luck, my father!'

Chapter Ten

There was a long silence. Nefaurau broke it. 'Father said I am to trust you. I have just a glimpse of you. As he imparted, I am not used to dealing at a level such as this.'

Sara walked towards Nefaurau. 'It is alright. You are still very young. A lot still to learn – especially about us.'

Nefaurau scuttled backwards, causing her to stop in her tracks. 'What is your problem with us?' she asked.

Cal was viewing this situation, seemingly detached; but he suddenly moved forward, standing now between Sara and the boy. He faced Sara and shook his head, at which she said, 'Oh, fuck you too. Bloody men! Even as boys they're the same. Hope I am expecting a girl!' She turned on her heel and found a seated position.

'No way for a lady to speak – especially in front of a child!' Cal was now pretty cross, and surprised at what he could muster up when roused enough. He turned towards Nefaurau, who was visibly shaking. Jesus, he thought, what do I say? But he managed to find words. 'Sara means well. It's just her way. Your dad – I mean, your father – is on a very important mission. I wish it could be me. I always wanted to be that useful.'

The boy looked straight at Cal. The stare was powerful. Too much so for Cal, who had to avert his eyes, casting them down to his feet as usual.

But there was a surprise in store for him. 'Deference is good. I will trust you as a friend from this very strange and hostile world.' Nefaurau moved past Cal back to a position between the pair. 'My father cares for things unknown to me amongst your kind. I know from what my mother has said to me that he blames himself for all that has occurred here. But my own mind on this is of a blame lying elsewhere. This is why I am here. There is one here I wish to address. And I *will* have my say.'

'Nefaurau, your father asked us both to look after you. Please do not take any action to prevent us completing his wishes. *Please!*' Sara was on her feet again.

'Calvin, Sara, I have much respect for what you are asking. But this abomination of existence must be dealt with.' Nefaurau made to leave.

'Do you not think your father is not, at this precise moment, about to strike at the same target as you are talking about? You could seriously jeopardise your father's intentions. You might even get him killed.' Cal's hands were clasped together in front of him pleading. '*Please*, please, Nefaurau. With utmost respect to you.'

Nefaurau stood quite still for several minutes, not looking at either of them. Then he sat down. With his back to them both.

Cal and Sara walked towards each other and hugged in triumph. So relieved. But the relief was tempered by the knowledge that they were dealing with a force of nature. Nefaurau was still the son of Djumbola, with all the possible implications such a connection could bring!

Djumbola had reached the suburbs. He didn't want to get too close. Not yet. He sat in the shadows. He watched the building gradually emptying. He had attired himself in a suit salvaged from his now trashed living quarters. Obviously not thinking it possible he would dare return, a lot more was left undisturbed.

The building security changed shifts. There were smiles on the faces of the departing day crew, leaving the grim personas of the night shift. Djumbola was happy with what he saw. The night crew were sufficiently known to him and they were far from the ultra-enthusiastic and efficient force such an assignment warranted. But, as the now revitalised Donald Gordon considered, you pays in peanuts, you gets your monkeys.

Don waited for all to settle into the normal rhythm of static security. The patrols went off leaving just the one guy manning the reception desk. Don entered through the main doors. The guard he knew well and showed no surprise at his arrival. Good, he'd be unaware of the goings-on earlier. Maybe they weren't even expecting me to return here, so didn't bother updating the security. 'Hi Jim. How's it going? Still having trouble with that back of yours?'

Jim Jackson: sixty-five years of living misery and complaints. If it wasn't his back it was at his front. If not his head it was lower down. 'Oh, not so bad now, Don. Thanks for asking. But my left ankle keeps swelling up.'

'Gout, Jim. First signs.'

Jackson looked up from his newspaper. 'You really think so? Christ, better make an appointment with my doctor. What do you think?'

'Think that's the way to go Jim.' Gordon was by now over by the lifts, having summoned an upwards car. Leaning casually against the wall, he tapped patiently on a trouser pocket. The lift arrived and Don Gordon disappeared inside.

Jackson went back to his paper. An internal buzzer sounded. A patrol calling in. 'Hey Jim. Lift to the ninth has been activated. Anyone we should know about?'

'Get back to your card game, Charlie. I am on the desk. Am I gonna let someone through who isn't kosher? Just a usual guy for that floor. No problems.'

'Okay, Jim. Keep what's left of your head on your shoulders. See you about five. Okay, buddy?'

'You want me to wake you then?' Jim was now completing the paper's crossword.

'So kind. Your turn tomorrow, huh?' Charlie didn't wait for a reply. The line went dead.

Jackson was halfway through the word game when the revolving door buzzer activated again. 'Ah, Mr Coney. How are you tonight? Much going on?' Jackson's newspaper was now lying on the floor. This son of a bitch can see round corners, Jackson thought. Fucking rattlesnake...

George Coney grunted something inaudible and pressed for a lift to the ninth. Then Jackson suddenly remembered. 'Mr Coney, sorry to bother you but I have a package here addressed to you, marked "Urgent".' He lifted the brown envelope in the air.

Coney sighed and re-emerged from the lift. Jackson was already outside the reception desk, not risking Coney getting too close to spotting the paper. Coney snatched the envelope from his hand and disappeared back into the lift just as the doors were closing.

'Well, thank you, Jim; or even Jackson. Son of a bitch! No manners. Not like that Don Gordon,' Jim muttered to himself.

By this time the internal buzzer was going like crazy. Jim made the connection and didn't wait for Charlie to start ranting. 'Okay, Charlie. Got us a snake on the ninth. George Coney. Keep your wits about you.'

'Jesus, Jim. Was nearly having a coronary here. Better take a look down there, huh? Show my face and all that. We know what a sneaking rat that one is. Let you know when it's done.'

Coney looked at the packet as the lift ascended. There were no markings of where it had been sent from. Just his name, and marked 'Urgent' in red. He decided to open it when he reached the office. The lift opened at the ninth but Coney took the stairs, climbing to the tenth floor. He entered a plush office and sat down at the desk.

George Coney often visited the building out of hours. That is why security were always jumpy when he arrived, thinking he was spying on their activity – or lack of it! He had been summoned away earlier to identify a prisoner held at a police station on the other side of town. With that completed, he had returned and was now, as always on his nocturnal visits, making himself comfortable in his immediate boss's office. Not a spying trip; just in need of a boost with delusions of grandeur.

He had temporarily forgotten about the package, and, reaching into an unlocked drawer, helped himself to one of the expensive cigars kept there by his boss – who, strangely, did not smoke himself. He just had them handy in case of a visit from his superiors, most of whom did like a good cigar! Coney removed the end and lit up, puffing a huge smoke ring towards the ceiling. He leant back, feet up on the desk; but being careful about marking its expensive veneer, he had removed his shoes beforehand. George was a pushy type. A member of the same lodge as his boss, he had hoped on promotion if he stuck close enough to him. Like a second skin. Not just for rapid rises within the ranks of employment but even more so to be amongst the throng in the hallowed halls of power. His ultimate was for a Governor's nomination. And then, who knows. Unfortunately, he was really unaware of his popularity rating – or severe lack of it. He was due to be making a speech at the lodge on the merits of the Security Services. Always made him sweat. Standing up in front of those who he felt were lesser mortals than himself. He wished them all to disappear into the ether, to leave him prominent. He had cut many corners to achieve this status thus far. He did, however, wonder how much they knew about his shady past.

Don Gordon had watched George Coney return to the building from an office on the ninth. Don had, of course, anticipated this, knowing a great deal about Coney's night-time habit. On top of this, he now knew where he obtained those garish fur hats from! Hearing the lift arrive on the ninth floor, Don waited a minute or so and then followed Coney's route up to the tenth. Gordon crept over to the opposite side of the floor to the office Coney had entered and sat down in a chair, hidden by the gloom. He watched as a young suit hesitantly walked over the expensive carpeted flooring – appearing to be unsure whether to knock on the office door. Don thought to himself, the shit is definitely in flight. Fan, strike one!

Agent Larry Fuller was a fairly clean-cut, normal kind of security agent. He hadn't meant to get so close. But she had given him a mighty come-on today. Fuller's main prioritised function was to stringently check the computer security system on an hourly basis. For this he worked a twelve-hour shift, sharing the total twenty-four-hour day with another agent. It could be pretty boring stuff. So with such an opportunity arising, he made the fatal decision of a grope in an empty office with a secretary instead of completing that particular hourly check. In fact, it went much further than a grope. A session of two hours! Meaning, he had experienced a wonderful time but had also missed a second check. His prick was still throbbing at the thought of another bout with her. But this sensation was being thoroughly messed up by the anxiety of an horrendous discovery – a nightmare caused by his own version of a fatal attraction! Sweat poured from his armpits through his suit jacket.

Coney, still puffing away merrily suddenly remembered the envelope. He reached for it, tearing a top end open. 'What is so fucking urgent about this shit?' He had first of all pulled out what appeared to be a miniature version of a hangman's noose. He peered inside. All that remained was a piece of paper, which had been folded several times. Coney sighed, believing it now to be some kind of practical joke. He could think of many who would fit the bill as such pranksters. He began to open the paper up. As he unravelled it he loudly coughed and spluttered, exhaling the smoke he had just inhaled, dropping the cigar at the same time. In complete shock he focussed on the photocopied image of the front cover of a magazine. The one taken from his cabinet. A cryptic message beneath this picture asked a simple question. 'The Hangman asks: Your place or mine?'

Fuller was about to knock. Hesitated. And in that moment heard Coney coughing loudly. Fuller recoiled a few paces and waited. Still summoning up the courage to knock on the door; dreading it. He had terrible disconcerting news. How much of it would be his fault for not noticing earlier was yet to be established. No, he couldn't make himself feel any better with that thought. It would definitely be the high jump for him.

Don Gordon heard the noise coming from within the office. He smiled and whispered to himself, 'George, you really have got to give up that filthy habit!' He watched the agent back off. Then moments later he returned and this time connected with a couple of raps upon the door.

Coney composed himself best he could, not expecting to be disturbed. 'Who is it?'

Fuller identified himself, and Coney, more with relief than anything else – and most unlike him – did not utter an oath back at him.

'Larry, come in. What can I do for you?'

George was now on his stockinged feet holding the office door open. Fuller disappeared inside the door, closing it behind him.

'What's that smell, sir?' Fuller's nose was wrinkling.

'Oh, just having a puff or two on the old cigar, you know.' Coney still being overfriendly; too friendly for Fuller's liking. But it was better his being in a good frame of mind with what he had to impart. But that smell?

'No, sir. Smells like burning.' Fuller looked down beside the chair Coney had just launched himself out of.

A plume of smoke was rising. George noticed it at the same time and stamped on the offending fire-raiser. Forgetting his shoes were elsewhere than on his feet, Coney stifled a squeal as the hot ash burnt through his sock. 'There – it's out now. No further problem,' he said through gritted teeth. His toes and sole were testimony to that being a damned lie! And the hole burnt in the expensive carpet... wasn't a thing George wanted to think about. Enough problems for one day.

'So what was it that is so damned important for you to disturb me, Fuller?' Coney was back to his usual.

Larry Fuller gulped and stammered out as best he could a situation report. 'Sir. We have a – a major problem. Maximum security.'

Coney looked at Fuller, not really hearing him properly. A second shock in as many minutes. First the magazine in his face, then the fucking cigar burning his foot. Now someone was trying to completely ruin his day.

'Calm it, son. What's so urgent? Nothing can be that important at this time of night, surely.' Then he suddenly had a cold sweat pour over him. He listened Fuller out, but he was somewhere else in his mind at the same time. Remembering suddenly... his office... his bureau. The magazine was in there. *And the fucking file*!

'Sir, umm, I ran the normal checks earlier. I went back for the replies and the system won't let me back in. It doesn't recognise the usual code numbers or words.' He gulped and felt he was going to spew.

George Coney still hadn't taken in the gravity of what Fuller was telling him. 'Are you alright, son? You are looking very pale.'

'Sorry, sir, I am going to be sick. Please excuse me.' Fuller started to leave, but Coney called to him to stand still.

'What do you mean, it won't let you back in? The codes wouldn't have been changed without my knowledge. Are you sure you punched in the right ones?' '

Fuller couldn't give him a reply, he was busy throwing up on the carpet!

'Jesus fucking Christ!' Coney was now really annoyed!

Fuller wiped his mouth and managed to say. 'I am sorry, sir. I used exactly the same set as usual. None of them are being recognised now.'

Coney's face now was red with fury, but Fuller hadn't noticed this. He was fleeing across the floor towards the nearest toilet facilities. He collided with Charlie, the security guard, on the way. The strange, overwhelming smell of burnt pork, combined with cigar smoke and spew, hit Charlie, even in his dazed condition. Fuller did not wait to offer an explanation. He was continuing his flight to the bathroom.

Charlie rose up from his enforced seated position on the floor and walked toward the open office door. Coney was out of it and closing the door before Charlie could reach it. 'It's okay, constable. Everything is being attended to. Just a slight mishap I will attend to personally. Now I am sure you have other matters to see to, huh?'

Charlie looked confused. Here was *the* guy we all hate saying he would clear up the mess himself. He thought he should consider calling up Jim for advice. But again, it might stir up a hornets' nest, and Jim would slay him for getting him into that kind of mess so near to his retirement date. No. He wouldn't bother him.

'It is just that we have to file a report, Mr Coney, sir.' Charlie was going to add that he was not a constable, but again thought it might prejudice the situation.

'It is alright, I will fill in our own report which we can duplicate for your files. Will that be satisfactory? Or have you some other idea which will cause me more delay?'

Charlie shook his head, knowing it was definitely time to leave.

'Then a good night to you, officer,' George called after him.

Charlie kept on going, but really felt like turning back. Only so much sarcasm a guy can take.

Coney walked over to the toilet. He desperately needed a pee himself. Whilst relieving himself, he called to Fuller, who was still managing to chunder – but mostly bile by this time. 'How for fuck's sake, *how*?'

Fuller emerged from a cubicle and muttered, 'Sabotage, maybe?'

'Sabotage? Who the fuck could have done that? This is supposed to be a completely secure maximum security site. When did you discover this fault?' Coney was zipping himself up.

Fuller was hoping Coney wouldn't ask that, but knew it would all come out when the timings were checked; although only the perpetrator would know when the codes were changed, and he wouldn't be likely to be coming back to inform on him.

'Only a matter of minutes ago, sir. It took me a while to find you.'

Another lie, but Coney wasn't to know that the whole night shift from Fuller himself down to Jim and his friends knew his little secret! But Fuller wasn't yet clear of Coney probably just for the time being. But another problem arose. He was beginning to urinate. That strange sensation when one end of the body has been in trauma and the brain is now slow to respond in informing another part of an impending disaster! Fuller first noticed the warm sensation and on looking down noticed the front of his trousers becoming soaked. He rushed to a urinal, whipping out that trusty member which had earlier stood so proud. Now he watched the shrivelled up version emptying the last dregs into the drainage. He wished at this point he could follow the flow out of there – all the way down to the sewer!

'When you've finished pissing and crapping yourself, you better had get on to the specialists and get them down here asap. Tell 'em we have codes to break urgently!'

Fuller limped away as quickly as possible.

George Coney was the proud owner of a collection of memorabilia covering and dating back to the old Wild West of America. His bookshelves heaved with books on how it was won from the Native American peoples. As a child he had always dreamed of going back in time and being a cowboy or soldier or anybody who had had the right to kill an Indian. In a room which he always kept locked, even from the prying eyes of his wife, Coney had a collection of genuine Indian scalps. He had these indelicately placed on the walls with the dates and tribes imprinted on cards underneath each of them. All the specimens dated back to the nineteenth century, but he had gaps to fill and had found a website which catered for that need. Although at this present moment in time he was now thinking it was not the best idea he had ever had!

He had also some connections involved in Klan activity. And to add to the potentially concerned sensitivities of any civil rights activist, Coney kept old photographs of blacks being beaten and whipped – and even hangings. His affiliations to the KKK benefited that organisation on many occasions, with Coney able to provide vital information, including top secret surveillance records.

Don Gordon watched the events with much amusement. It was working out better than he could ever have expected. 'Roll up! Roll up! An extravaganza of comedic expertise. Starring our own and exalted George "Don't let the wig slip" Coney!' Don chuckled mirthfully to himself. Coney was now back in his office after ridding himself of proper security!

George Coney would have liked to sit down and cry. Surveying the scene in his boss's office he knew it was going to take some explanation. And there were witnesses to contradict anything he was likely to say. And the stench was overpowering. He went to the window, but the security locks were on. He tried to upgrade the level of air-conditioning but it wasn't responding. He was still thinking what next to do when the phone rang. Coney froze. He could feel the icy wind on his neck. He went to pick it up but then recoiled, as if it was an unexploded bomb. It rang off. Coney waited a few seconds and then exited, locking the office door behind him. He would clear up later. More pressing matters to contend with.

Don Gordon again was chuckling, having just replaced the telephone receiver on the desk beside him!

Coney rushed back down the stairs to the ninth. Entering his office, he immediately saw what was amiss. The drawers in his bureau were partially open. His worst fears were now reality. He peered into the gaps where the magazine and file had been stored. He even noticed that the 'hairpiece' had been moved. 'Jesus Christ! What the fuck do I do now?' he muttered to himself. The magazine was a bad enough discovery for whoever. But the file! It had everything in it. 'Oh why oh why did I take it out of there? Too late to fucking worry about that now.'

He began to gather up his papers, suddenly feeling an urgent need to leave. He went to open the door, but froze as it opened before him. He looked up and felt a wave of relief course through his system. There stood his reliable sidekick – Margaret Madison.

He was in need of another smoke. All he had in his desk drawer was a cheap panatella, but he chose to light this up. His chest heaved as he inhaled. He coughed and spluttered again; the residue of the previous trauma. Margaret pulled a face of complaint. 'George, you should give those things up. Not good for you.'

'Maybe the last fucking thing I ever will have the chance to give up! The whole fucking thing has gone crazy, Maddie. Someone has accessed the system and changed all the fucking codes. We have a definite rogue trader in this building.'

Madison was now all ears. 'Who, George? Who do you think it is?'

Coney was sweating profusely and letting off bad odour. 'Only one fucker I can think of, and he was here earlier. That fucker who set us up. Don Gordon.' Coney was still trying to work out why she had suddenly appeared. He didn't really trust *anyone* at this precise moment. His mind was on a racetrack, with his sanity as the winning prize!

'Jesus, George, I am still fucking getting over that. He is one mean fucking nigger! How *did* he manage to get my panties on your head without either of us knowing?' Maddie cried.

'Some spooky shit coming out of that man. Fucking witch doctor. Voodoo and all that.' He had watched as she crossed over to the desk with that sashaying walk of hers. Her lithe body was tantalising. She just needed to be taken from behind, because the face could sink a thousand erections! But even given the circumstances he was in, the image of her body could still do things to him. He was getting aroused. She sat on the desk right in front of him. Her right foot went straight to his private area. Toying with it.

'Jesus, Maddie. I always believed there might be something else other than our professional expertise. Just didn't expect it quite at this moment. For Christ's sake, he might have done for us all!'

She kept the pressure on his dick. 'Poor baby. Let Maddie see if she can make her little friend feel better. Would little Georgie like that? Shall I ask him?'

Coney was very confused about what she had just said, but despite it he was nodding, his base instincts taking over.

Maddie Madison was now living up to her mad cow name. She bent down and kissed him on the lips. She had obviously been hitting the bottle, as her breath reeked of alcohol.

'Jesus, Maddie. Are you drunk?'

Maddie paused, then most unlike her, giggled! 'Oh, come on, George. Little tipsy maybe. But a little drink can do wonders. All I see at the moment is some gorgeous guy who wants me to suck him off!'

She got on her knees, unzipping George's fly, and pulled at the front of his pants. His prick sprang out, striking her formidable nose. She squeaked an oath. 'Fuck you, that hurt!' Then giggled again. 'Am I not a naughty girl, Georgie?'

She proceeded to put it in her mouth and bit on it. Now it was George's turn to cry out oaths! But he soon quietened down to contented gurgles and groans as Maddie went about the business.

Don Gordon rose quietly and walked over to the office door, which was still half open. He watched the action, thinking to himself what a weird bunch of people inhabited these close confines. Here was he expecting them to be panicking. None of it made sense to him. But she was definitely a 'mad cow' – and George, well, not the full ticket!

It was time to go and find out happenings in pastures new. He was sensing something wrong, but couldn't pinpoint it.

Chapter Eleven

The telephone rang in a room, no ordinary room, for it was full of extremely expensive artefacts. A collection put together over many years. A collector proud of his ability to sound out the ultimate unique item. Not for him anything anyone else possessed. On the rare occasions when he discovered someone else had a copy, he would pursue it until it fell into his hands. Whatever the cost. Then destroy it! To keep a uniqueness.

'Mr XChiang. An update. We pursued the item of your instructions. He somehow escaped our full attention, leaving a pile of clothes at the scene. A naked Blackman somewhere should have provided a positive sighting – even a clue.'

XChiang was silent for a moment. 'Can anything yet be traced back to the committee?'

'Mr XChiang. Please. We are very thorough and usually on top of things.'

XChiang frowned on the 'usually'. 'And *usually* being on the top of things, you will let me know if there are any other developments?'

'Mr XChiang, we are the best in the business. You employ us because of this. If anything arises to complicate our professional relationship it will be dealt with as usual.'

'Good man. Fantastic. I am very pleased with your efforts so far. Please update me as soon as you have news of our elusive Blackman. Thank you again.' XChiang moved with stealth towards another open line. 'You have listened to that?'

'We have.'

'Recommendations?'

'All will have to be eventually eliminated.'

'All?' XChiang was confused.

'No margin for error. And we have a problem.'

XChiang was now aware things weren't going well! 'Tell me. No holding back. That is our deal.'

'A name we have come across. *Nefaurau*.'

'Yes, yes. But you have already pointed this out to me.'

'His mother is Sahariah, and father appears to be a Djumbola. These have been circulated in the usual channels. The specialists have picked up on the importance in their own world. Ancient priests. Does this make any sense to you, Mr XChiang?'

'Yes, of course. But please get to the point.' XChiang had to use all his powers of restraint not to cry out in anguish, *Djumbola*!

But the unexpected news was to become worse. 'Djumbola is already here. He is a Donald Gordon in this life.'

XChiang was not expecting this. But inscrutability being his heritage, his voice bore not the hint of concern. 'Thank you. Your usual fee. And a bonus will be forwarded to the usual account. Goodnight.'

As he replaced the receiver, XChiang smashed everything in his sight. The noise brought his own personal security rushing into the room. XChiang was sitting amongst the debris. Eyes fixed on a ring. Third finger. Left hand. He was muttering indistinguishably. Vaguely aware of the presence of his most highly respected guards, he merely waved them away. After looking at each other for brief seconds in bewilderment, they then departed. Neither had witnessed anything like it in many years of service to XChiang.

In another room a telephone rang. XChiang's personal assistant answered the call. His master would be resting after all those exertions. His assistant *had* seen XChiang in such a fury before. Those who angered him on that occasion had been dealt with by his personal elite 'Ghost Squad'. Combining many qualities of the ninja with other deadly skills, they were always in preparation for the next assignment. Hungry. Totally focussed on terminating the next subject. Always clearing up all possible links to their master.

'I need to talk to Mr XChiang. Very urgent. No, extremely urgent.'

'Who may I ask is enquiring after the health of my master, please?' Tongue in very much cheek!

Beginning to sound more agitated, the voice on the other end of the line spat, 'You know well who I am and who I represent, you cheap Chink fuck. Get him on this fucking line *now*.'

The assistant jumped. Not from the ferocity of the voice on the line, but XChiang had taken over the receiver from his hand. Covering the mouthpiece, XChiang whispered, 'Have to see about your earwax, Lin So!' His personal assistant tapped XChiang's cheek lightly with a finger, which induced a huge smile. On both faces.

Mimicking his assistant, 'Sorry. So, sorry. Mistah XChiang not available. Perhaps you want fried duck instead? Or even fried luck?'

'Are you taking the piss? Get that fucking slant-eyed bitch in heat of yours on this line *now*!'

'That is very irreverent, Mr Steinburg. You are he, I presume correctly, no?' said XChiang, still mimicking Lin So.

'Of course it is. What the fucking hell have I got say to get your ass moving in the right direction and bring your master back to this phone?'

'Perhaps my master does not need to be called. Maybe he might already be here listening to your rants.'

There was no reply.

'Perhaps, my friend, you need to fuck a fried duck. Or take a serious rain check on your luck!'

Silence on the other end of the line. XChiang could almost imagine how much Steinburg must be kicking himself, red in the face and extremely unhappy, obviously realising he had been seriously compromised. And Steinburg being Coney's immediate superior, it appeared to XChiang that such abuse was a necessity within that power structure to be successful and acceptable to the others. And it included a very bad attitude when dealing with anything outside the white race.

'Well, Mr Steinburg, now the formalities of identifying ourselves are established, can we please stop wasting each other's time and get to the point of your call. Please.' XChiang was loving the thought of a major one-up on his greasy so-called ally. He stuck with any of them only because of their use in his plan. But Steinburg and his cohorts were fast losing ground.

'So it is you there now, XChiang?' Steinburg started to bluster, obviously trying to establish a more convivial conversation. 'We have a major problem. The codes on the system have been changed. We can't access the damned thing. Got the code breakers on it at the moment. They will inform me as soon as this has been achieved.'

XChiang was silent for a few moments.

'Did you hear me, XChiang?'

'Yes, Mr Steinburg, I have heard you. But there must be more than that to tell. After all, the system is very efficient and I cannot believe for a moment it would change its code workings without first telling me!'

'Oh. Ha, ha, Mr XChiang! But this isn't a time for flippancy. If the fucker who got into the system knew enough to change the codes, what else could he have been up to?'

'Well, Mr Steinburg, you still have not been able to elucidate me enough on this matter. Are you covering something up? Is a member of your staff responsible for this sabotage?' Lin So and XChiang were now nodding to each other. His assistant left the room to make another call elsewhere.

'Look, Mr XChiang, I have just this minute come off the phone to the specialists. That is all they were able to give me.' XChiang could smell the rat surfacing.

'*All*? What about your main man George Coney?'

'Er, he's there at the building at the moment, directing operations.' Steinburg was sounding more and more agitated.

'With respect, Mr Steinburg, your compatriot, George Coney, could not direct an apple into his mouth without it first landing in his ear! I would respectively advise you to get your own ass down there immediately and report back to me as soon as you have any fresh information. Is that clear?'

Steinburg coughed to disguise the oaths issuing in whispers involuntarily from his mouth. XChiang made some of them out but chose to ignore them. 'Is that clear to you, Mr Steinburg? I will expect a report back within the next hour.'

Through gritted teeth, Steinburg acknowledged his brief and the line went dead.

'Well, thank you for your call Mr Steinburg. I hope very much to be enjoying your company again in the very near future,' XChiang said to the now dead connection.

Lin So returned to the room. XChiang embraced him and began to shake. 'I have a great fear over this, Lin So. My senses tell me another maybe more powerful than me is already here wreaking havoc with all my good intentions.' He kissed Lin So briefly on the lips then took his leave.

As he reached the doorway, Lin So called after him. 'I have put into operation what was required. The squad are even now making their way to the spot you said may be his point of entry again.'

XChiang stopped, but did not look around. In a very quiet and subdued voice, he thanked Lin So.

Chapter Twelve

Cal was the first to awaken. He stretched, looking across at the heaped bundle which should have been the sleeping Nefaurau. Something didn't look right. Odd shape. Cal was on his feet so quickly that he lost his balance and sat down again with a thud. Pulling himself up again, he grunted, alerting Sara's senses. She lifted herself up on one elbow. 'What now, Cal. Sleepwalking?'

Cal was in no mood, having hurt his backside in the fall. His equilibrium was still a little wayward but his eyesight for once wasn't playing tricks on him. 'Not me who is sleepwalking, Sara. Look.' He pointed at the increasingly improbable bundle representing a sleeping Nefaurau. Both stood now over the remnants of a child's trick.

'Christ, what now?' Cal asked. But Sara had no answer. Just stared at the empty bed.

The pair sat opposite each other drinking a third cup of coffee each. It seemed like ages. But waiting like this for something to happen always did. Suddenly, out of the gloom Nefaurau appeared. He sauntered into the hut and started warming his hands on the fire.

Cal leapt to his feet. 'Where the hell – I mean, I'm sorry. But where the... Where have you been? We have been worried. No, not just worried. Beside ourselves.'

Nefaurau looked at him with eyes wide. Perhaps he had never experienced anyone shouting like that at him.

'Shut up, Cal. *Shut up!*' Sara was bristling again with protective womanhood. But with this difficult child it was nigh impossible, she thought. 'Nefaurau. You promised us. On the pain of the possibility of you causing a huge problem for your father.'

Nefaurau merely waved a hand. 'My father's affairs are his own. This place is not far or wide enough for one such as me.'

For a split second, Sara lost that initial feeling of protectiveness. She seriously felt like giving the royal child a clip around the ear. An erstwhile child in need of a leathering. Cal saw the change of mood in her and put an arm around her. He managed to restrain her but his reward for saving the day was a serious bruise! Before Cal could manage a protest at the latest injury, a blinding flash sat him on his backside again. And that did hurt!

The pair were to debate the situation afterwards, playing it back over and over again. They differed in their interpretations. Cal had seen figures in devil masks in combat with the cloaked and hooded ones. But Sara had seen a dragon devouring many lions, only for a tiger to bite the dragon's tail.

'What were you on, Sara? Definitely not... much simpler than that,' Cal said shaking his head.

'We were fed some pretty good dope, hey, Cal?'

He looked at her and began to feel some concern. Sara was showing signs of severe intoxication. Boss-eyed... speech slurred... not making any sense at all!

Cal was so intent on Sara's ramblings he missed another's presence. Sara was first to notice. 'Hey, kiddo! The man is back,' she remarked, and giggled – a most unlikely sound, coming from her.

Djumbola stood before them. Not looking at all happy. 'Nefaurau?'

'Don't know. Hic!' was Sara's only response.

'Is she sick? Or have you managed to find intoxicants? Wished for them?' Djumbola's glare was most disconcerting for one of them. But the other couldn't care less, given the state she was in!

'Djumbola, before you start getting angry with us, remember Nefaurau has a mind of his own.' Cal was waiting for him to explode. But Djumbola seemed to take the point.

'I know that. What else occurred?'

'We woke up this morning. He had disappeared. Then some time later he just wanders in. We have a go at him over letting you down and all that. He just gives the impression that this place isn't big enough for one such as him. That's the way he put it.'

Djumbola nodded in agreement. 'So please go on, Calvin. I am sure what happened next will not surprise me in the least, as I am aware of where he went and why.'

Cal looked a little uneasy now, not sure whether to continue in the circumstances.

'It is fine, Calvin. I have not a problem with the pair of you. As you have said, my son, like his father – and mother, I would add – has a tendency to go his own way on things. Please continue, Calvin.'

He was a little more reassured, but still edgy. 'Well, soon after he wanders in, this Chinese army in devil masks arrives and battles with your hooded friends. Sara saw it a bit differently. A dragon – eating lions. Then a tiger turns up and is biting the dragon's tail. Huh? What kind of trip is that?'

'Simple to explain, Calvin. As in dream interpretation. You witnessed a half-reality. Sara witnessed a whole but in cryptic version. I will have to dwell on both. I take it neither of you know what happened to Nefaurau. Any demands for release and such?'

'Uh-uh! No. Suppose that is the case with me. But I don't know about Sara. She's not making much sense at the moment. I have been a little concerned about her.'

'It is to be expected. You are a couple. A very recent pairing. You both still have a lot to learn about each other. But that will come in time. I think Sara will have more to give us when she is awake again.' Djumbola turned away and wandered off.

Cal took this opportunity to try and sober Sara up. He sat beside her, cajoling. Sensing something must be important, she partially came to. Djumbola turned back at the sound of her voice.

'Hi, Djumbola. Long time no see.' Her eyes were hardly focussing. 'Still got that big, erm, thingy!' Again she began to giggle. Definitely not a sober Sara!

Djumbola looked at Cal. 'It's going to be a long night, Calvin. But I will wait here. When she can make sense, please bring this news to me.'

Cal was beside himself by now. 'Yes sir.' Then Cal thought to himself – Big thing?

He was quickly brought out of that reverie. 'Calvin, lighten up with this "Sir" shit. Okay, buddy?'

Cal nodded back. He could see that Djumbola was extremely unhappy with the situation, but could still find time to make such a light reply. To Cal he was an okay kind of guy! As if reading his mind, Djumbola winked at him and then went to put his own head down. Not his preferred choice, but the agenda was hiccuping with Sara!

George Coney was standing in the main foyer chatting to the security staff when Steinburg emerged through the swing doors. All attention reverted to him.

Steinburg first focussed on Coney. 'You – upstairs now! You other fuckers, I want a report as of now. Well, George? Are you going upstairs to wait for me?'

Coney had hesitated, as if having unfinished business to attend to, but he gave a nod to show his understanding of what he had to do. But he was most obviously reluctant to leave at that moment.

'Mr Steinburg, sir. I think there may be a few matters we need to discuss before I go upstairs.' Coney had a look of the ultimate haunted man.

'George, I have nothing more to add. Please make your way up to the tenth floor and I will see you there.' Steinburg's eyes were on the security crew.

Jim Jackson was not shy in noticing this. As Coney disappeared in the lift he made his feelings known. 'Mr Steinburg, if there is something wrong going on in this building, it is definitely not anything to do with my boys. They may not have the wherewithal of those who they are supposedly protecting, but I would give up my pension rights if I thought even one of them was not doing his job right.'

'And what makes you think I would be any different in that assessment, Jim?' Steinburg was eyeing Jackson with some suspicion.

Jim had to make a decision now. He was being asked to be a whistle-blower just a matter of days from his retirement on full pensionable rights. The rest of his night crew were watching him closely.

'Well, for a start-off he asked us not to bother with our own report about the fire. That he would fill in his own report and give us a copy. Which he hasn't.'

'I am hearing you. And it is a very serious accusation, Jim. So where was the fire?'

Jackson looked surprised at the question. 'You mean you do not know, Mr Steinburg? I thought it was the reason you were here.'

Steinburg now was beginning to get angry. 'Why the fuck should I be called out for a fire in the building? Others are here for that.'

'Well, I just thought as it occurred in your office—'

Steinburg cut him short. '*My* office? How the hell did that happen? Who the hell was in there?'

'George Coney, sir.' Jim Jackson was loving this now. He could see Coney had not even told his boss yet. Fireworks were the order of the day!

Steinburg made as if to leave the reception desk, snorting furiously and heading for the lifts. Jackson called after him. 'Oh, Mr Steinburg, by the way, that nice man Donald Gordon advised us to fill our own report in and he countersigned it as a witness.'

Steinburg whipped around to face Jackson again. 'Gordon? Here in the building? He witnessed the fire?'

'Yes, that's correct, sir. Very helpful, I must say.' Jim was trying hard not to give his feelings away too much. Seeing Steinburg's reaction to the news just made his day!

Steinburg turned tail again and entered the elevator, pressing for the tenth. He was glaring back at the security crew as the doors were closing. Once gone, Jim Jackson let out a whoop. The others were around him patting him on the back in congratulations. Charlie exclaimed, 'See you didn't pass on Don's good wishes to Steinburg, as he asked you to!'

They all hooted with laughter. When Jim had recovered from this he replied, 'Don't think that son of a bitch could take anymore. Coney's in for a real treat. Wish we were up there to watch!' This remark caused more mirth amongst them.

As the lift doors opened on the tenth floor, Steinburg could see his office door ajar. He walked over and pushed it open further to find Coney on his hands and knees scrubbing the carpet with a hard brush. A pail of soapy water stood beside him.

Steinburg spoke, causing Coney to leap off the floor to a standing position. 'What the fucking hell is going on, George? I have been called away from a most important Masonic gathering, firstly to be insulted by that Chinese prick, XChiang. Had to have the honour of informing him of this monumental cock-up here. And now I find my office carpet burnt – and what's that other fucking smell?'

'Puke, sir. Larry Fuller spewed when reporting to me that the codes weren't working. He also made me drop my cigar, bursting in on me like that.' Coney was trying to maintain eye contact with Steinburg but failed to be convincing.

'But what were you doing in my office in the first place?' Steinburg was holding Coney in a steady stare.

'I–I, er, was looking for a file I mislaid. I wondered if you might have picked it up and brought it up here.' Coney was really making a mess of his excuses!

'What fucking file, George? What are you on about?' Steinburg, beginning to smell something really bad glared at Coney. Shit hitting a fan, he thought to himself.

'I know I was wrong to do it but I took a file from the vault down to my office for a quick perusal.' Coney was starting to sweat heavily. Deeper and deeper into the mire...

'What classification?' As if he needed to ask anything further. This stupid jerk was going to tell him it was a red code one. Not to be removed from the vault. And George Coney complied, although again trying to wriggle some way out of the full impact.

'I got a call for an urgent identification of a suspect on the other side of town. I know I should have whipped it back up to the vaults. But I thought it would be safe enough locked in my bureau until I got back. Only a matter of a couple of hours. But in that time the bureau had been forced and the file had gone.'

'Jesus fucking H! What is in that numb skull of yours? You just said you were in my office looking for it. Which way round is it now?' Steinburg was breathing heavily. He was becoming stressed with the thought of the next question.

Coney was about to answer but was cut short as Steinburg spat, 'Did the file have the code number for the system?' Coney was mouthing a reply but no sound was emitted.

'But obviously not the fucking code words! They are exclusive. Apart from XChiang himself, who obviously knows each of them, all are spread amongst the select few, who know one each and would only confer if something happened to XChiang. So someone seems to have got mighty lucky with his guesses. Or that fucking Chinaman is screwing us all off. Have you got any idea who might have taken the file?'

'I have. Donald Gordon. He was watching me reading the file. And was still here when I left. He must have watched me lock the file away.'

Steinburg looked stunned. Lost for words. Immersed for a moment in thought. 'You know he was here just now, don't you, George?'

Coney looked puzzled. 'I don't understand. What do you mean? Gordon was still here in the building?'

'Yes, George. He's signed the security report as a witness to the fire in my office. That means he must have been watching you the whole time. Probably from across the lobby.' Steinburg watched as Coney's whole disposition changed. He was ghostly white and his shoulders sagged.

'Oh my fucking God!'

'You can say that again, George. Now I have to report all this back to Chinky Sam. Then wait for the thunderstorm. I think you will need to disappear pronto, my friend. Knowing how XChiang works he will have assigned death warrants for anyone who fucked up over this.'

George Coney gulped. He was about to be sick.

'George, fuck off out of my office now. Go puke up whatever is waiting to appear. Then get your ass down to the lodge. I will arrange for some kind of safe house for you.'

Coney started to thank him but then retched. He sped across the lobby now, heading for the bathroom, his hand tightly over his gurgling mouth. Steinburg thought it appropriate. His hand over his mouth – always just a little too late. Coney had let go his vomit as he opened the bathroom door. It splashed back over his suit. Then he disappeared inside. Steinburg closed his office door and sat there reflecting about a telephone call he was dreading.

'Shit! Ouch – my head! Oh, my poor head. Oh no. *Noooooooooo!*' Sara's noisy sobbing woke Cal with a start. He shot onto his feet, tottering in the dance of a nowhere man!

Djumbola was already awake. He had been watching over Sara closely for quite some time. He had been concerned. There were certain signs only he would have noticed. Djumbola knew XChiang's potions tended to be potent. Some gave more or less a happy aftertaste. However, only when the illusions weren't sending the recipient half mad. Then there were those that had terrible withdrawal symptoms, often eventually proving fatal. Djumbola was convinced Sara had a dose of the latter. He could imagine why, especially given the scratches and bruising about her body. She had given them one hell of a fight before they took his son.

Cal slowly came to, registering the fact that Djumbola was tending to Sara. Djumbola had been feeding Sara concoctions, something Cal was glad he had not witnessed. Also sopping wet poultices for her infected wounds. Herbs and all manner of things laced with special dust. A grand concoction of mush. Stank to high heaven! No one in their right mind would consume it. But Sara was losing hers at one point, and Djumbola did not hesitate to feed her it. She had moaned loudly then and frequently throughout her fever; even sat bolt upright on one occasion, cursing everything in her sight at that very moment. Whoever was disturbing her then had better pray she didn't remember when she regained consciousness! Cal had slept through most of it but had stirred from time to time, obviously disturbed by the racket. This was not without the assistance of another of Djumbola's concoctions. He did not want Cal to be getting in the way. It was that serious.

Djumbola laid his hand on Sara's forehead. 'Feels good. Oh! That feels so good. So, so, cool. Lovely.'

Djumbola spoke quietly but in urgent tone. 'Sara, there is not much time. I need to know. The Chinese man came through that dream. The Lions and Dragon. And finally the Tiger. He said something to you but did not expect you to survive.'

'What?' Sara was still enjoying the coolness of touch.

'Dragon. Tiger on tail. Lions devoured. Remember? *Chinaman*. XChiang. Sara, please think. This man has taken Nefaurau. What did he say to you? Can you remember? It is vitally important, Sara.'

She looked very confused. Still dazed. Then suddenly she remembered. 'Oh God. I had hold of Nefaurau. They were pulling him away from me. So I let go and went at them. Too many for me. Bastards were kicking and punching and pouring this shit over me.'

Cal was looking bemused, not remembering anything about the episode. Sara looked across at him. She could see he was crestfallen. Had he been a coward? She could see it in the glance he gave her.

'It's okay, Cal. You were knocked unconscious.' Cal looked back now, very confused.

'You really don't remember, Cal?' He shook his head. 'Christ! They came from nowhere. You instinctively put yourself in front of them, guarding Nefaurau and me. Silly sod! That's why your dream was different to mine. I saw more.'

'Sara, you can have this conversation with Cal when I am gone. Please try to remember what he said to you.' Djumbola made a gesture to Cal and he sat down.

Sara started to bristle. 'Don't you put my man down! He did his best. Not everyone can be what that fucking Arnie is supposed to be. Worst fucking non-believable hero on film. And now he's a fucking politician. Just great. A political non-hero. *Yuuuurrk*!'

'Okay, I get your message, Sara. But Nefaurau is out there now. Only with a slim chance of survival. I know XChiang. I know his methods. If he practises them on my son I promise I will make this world *dust*!'

Cal came into his own at this point. 'Sara, please try and remember what and who we are. Who Djumbola is. Who Nefaurau is. And who Sahariah is – his mother. I know you, Sara, at least that much. You would never forgive yourself if he were terribly harmed. And the chances of that are increasing all the time.'

Well said, Calvin, Djumbola had in his thoughts. He looked at Sara, who was returning the stare. 'I realise you are not yet fully recovered from what they did to you. I will wait a little while longer to aid that recovery. Blessings be to you both.'

Djumbola then did his usual trick and disappeared.

Cal looked at Sara. She was not a happy bunny! 'What is all

this drama with you men? I was about to tell him what he said. That horrible vile Chinese worm. He said he was going to bugger Nefaurau himself when the mood took him.'

'Then why didn't you tell Djumbola that?' Cal asked.

'Because he already knew. He read it in my eyes. I knew he had read it in my eyes. I wasn't going to give him anything more. Sahariah said he can be the ultimate bastard.'

Cal was now even more confused than ever. '*Sahariah?*'

'Cal, you are a mere man. Whatever this world has evolved into, man remains the fucking same. You want to be fed and fucked. Not necessarily by the same entity. But there we are. Man is in charge of proceedings here. A woman would change it. I just have a feeling Sahariah and me would get on – big time!'

Cal was now pretty upset. 'Sara, you have a high ideal on it. But you have just caused Djumbola to go out there looking for his son without him knowing what you know about it. Sahariah would not be happy about that.'

Sara looked down. 'Cal, the truth is I can't remember anything much about it. I just hope the dreams made some sense to him.'

'He didn't realise I was still conscious. He plied me with this smelly stuff to drink down. But I spat it out when he turned away. I made out I was sleeping but watched him. He saved you, Sara, by what he did... the perseverance, the patience required. You were a tough cookie for him to save, Sara.'

Sara seemed to be staring into an empty space as Cal talked. She came out of it to exhort on herself. 'That Chinaman was taking Nefaurau to a meeting. As a trophy. To stop them. A mutiny.' Cal sat back, astonished by her sudden recall.

'Thank you, Sara! All is now revealed,' said a voice.

They both looked around. Djumbola was not in evidence. He had been standing just outside of their sight listening intently. He was more aware now of XChiang's plan. But he still had to trace the meeting.

Chapter Thirteen

Nelson Horatio Steinburg sat in his office debating about the impending call he had to make. He knew that XChiang would immediately smell a rat, and George Coney would be on the list for termination. It was not for professional reasons he was intending to spirit Coney away, but more for what George could reveal about Steinburg's activities if he began to spill the beans; which he would be sure to do if cornered. The Klan were George's friends for services he had rendered. Steinburg swam in murky waters, but not near those sharks. He had his own connections in the underworld: drug barons; Mafia; splinter groups. All sitting on the periphery of Masonic dealings. Steinburg himself was a pretty high up member of this society and so could pull quite a few strings, all round.

He was christened 'Nelson Horatio' after the famous admiral, his family believing they were distantly related to him. Where they got that idea from no one really knew, but it had become so fashionable to talk in terms of its probability it was latterly taken as fact. Steinburg absolutely loathed the names. He never encouraged anyone to use them except at important Masonic gatherings where they seemed to enhance his standing. And he certainly didn't mind that! However, he had recently let slip the Christian names at a security advisory function after a couple of glasses of wine too many. He had later overheard his nickname – 'Mandela' – being used, and was absolutely livid. Referring obviously to Nelson Mandela, who would have been the very last person Steinburg would ever invite to his club. Steinburg was the same as George Coney in this one aspect at least. He hated anybody black, red or yellow, and saw them as inferior. And he had a special loathing for Donald Gordon. He was thinking a lot about him at the moment. Just how far had that man gone when he had broken the codes? And that damned file! Jesus, it had so much sensitive information inside it. In the wrong hands it did not bear thinking about...

Steinburg decided to contact the special code breakers who were busy in the main systems room on the fourteenth floor. It wasn't good news thus far. He was informed of the probability that each time they entered a wrong code it could be encouraging whatever was inside it to strike at a faster rate. Like bating a rattlesnake with a stick. Steinburg just asked them to keep him informed.

He then made a cail to a large mansion on a distant island in the tropics. The recipient of this call had informed Steinburg that he would call back on a secure line. Steinburg's telephone rang, and even though he was expecting it he had jumped slightly. His nerves were starting to frazzle.

On the other end was billionaire Henry C *Weinstack*. His money had been made through many years of dealings in the same murky waters which found Steinburg and Coney swimming alongside; except that Weinstack could afford a luxury liner or two, whilst the other pair were rowing boat class!

Weinstack was not in the listings of richest men. He considered details of his wealth to be his own exclusive business and no one else's. The man was ultra-secretive and more reclusive than ten Howard Hugheses. Weinstack had fingers in so many pies. No, perhaps whole hands, arms, right up to the elbows, in every conceivable money-making venture. He saw consumers as weak and stupid. Easy to sell crap to. His motto: 'Sell it to 'em till they spew it back to us in dollars!' And there were the other less savoury dealings. Drug running, arms sales, prostitution and more shady connections than BT.

To run this massive organisation, Weinstack had a gallery of underlings. All hanging on his every whim. He was also of the same mind as Steinburg and Coney, but reserved his most hatred for anything Oriental. He was on record as considering that Hiroshima and Nagasaki should have been the prelude to the bombing out of the whole Far East. Including, of course, XChiang's homeland.

'Now what can I do for you, Nelson Ho?' It was just Weinstack's little attempt at humour. Yet another nickname. And sounding Oriental! Steinburg had to take it on the chin.

'Mr Weinstack. Firstly, sorry to contact you at this hour but we have had some strange goings-on here.' Steinburg was swallowing hard as he spoke.

'Like what, Steinburg? You do not sound your usual self. Hope it's not catching.' Weinstack allowed himself another chuckle at Steinburg's expense.

'Someone has managed to get into the system, broken our codes and replaced them with their own. We haven't been able to break them yet. Without this, we are unable to access the system to see what damage has been done.'

There was complete silence on the other end of the line. Steinburg was now very jumpy. The sweat began to appear on his brow. He reached inside his pocket for a handkerchief. He mopped his brow, waiting for the explosion!

Weinstack's mood had changed considerably but he did not rant and rave as expected. 'And XChiang? What does he know about this? After all, he was the only one with knowledge of all the relevant codes.'

'He has asked me to get back to him when I know more. But I am in agreement with your way of thinking, sir. XChiang could be the culprit in some way.'

Weinstack spat back, 'Do not ever presume to be in agreement with how I am thinking. No one I know has that privilege. Am I making myself clear, Steinburg?'

Steinburg winced. 'Yes sir. Fully understood. My apologies.'

'Accepted. I think this will necessitate a meeting of all our group. Will you be talking to XChiang?'

'It is my next call.'

'Good. Get him to arrange a meeting asap. Those who cannot attend in person – which of course, includes myself – will be expected to connect up on secure video link. Is all that clear?'

'Yes sir. That will be arranged.' Steinburg was now glad this conversation was about to end. He was in need of a toilet.

'Thank you and goodbye for now, Nelson Ho!' A further chuckle, then the line disconnected.

Steinburg leapt out of the chair, heading for the bathroom. He was too late in noticing the bucket of soapy water left behind by Coney. He tripped over it, sending the contents splashing over the already stained carpet. He threw out hands to halt the impact of his fall, but fingers slipped as he came down in the middle of the puke mark. He skidded onto his belly into the same mess, which was still wet and slippery, having only been partially cleaned up by Coney. Steinburg got to his feet and hissed oaths at imaginary culprits!

As he returned to the office the telephone rang. 'Mr Steinburg, I am most pleased that we are able to discuss the update of the matter in hand. Please forgive my bothering you again, but I was waiting patiently for your call and became just a little restless.'

'Apologies, Mr XChiang. I have been busy directing operations at this end. Still no success with the code breaking.'

'Also busy spiriting your friend George Coney away... and contacting Henry Weinstack before getting back to me.'

Steinburg froze. How did he know all that? Is my telephone bugged? Is the office bugged? In fact is the whole fucking building bugged? He tried not to panic.

'I just thought it appropriate to call Mr Weinstack under the circumstances, as he has the most to lose financially if the worst happens.'

'And what would be the worst scenario, Mr Steinburg?' XChiang was now very interested in the reply.

'Well, everyone knows what a virus can achieve. If this is the intention of whoever sabotaged the codes, then anything is possible. The whole of our system could be devoured and it will go looking for other connections to eat. Into banking systems, governmental offshoots – even space programmes. Anything connected in however small a capacity could be hit. Very serious implications.'

XChiang was silent. Not being at all technically minded and not having any desire to learn even rudimentary computer skills, he was totally unaware of this possibility. He was in complete shock. Lin So was standing close by and rushed forward as his master swayed towards a faint. Lin So grabbed the receiver and curtly spoke to Steinburg. 'This conversation ends. My master will be resting for the time being. Was there anything else of import before I disconnect?'

Steinburg faked concern. 'I am truly sorry if what I have just said has made Mr XChiang feel ill. Of course I will wait to hear back from him when he is feeling better. Only one other matter: Mr Weinstack has asked for a meeting of the group to discuss the problem.'

'That is already being arranged. My master first thought of this before Mr Weinstack interfered. I will say good day to you, Mistah Steinburg.' The line went dead.

Steinburg sat for a few moments mulling over the situation. Most unlike XChiang to keel over, unless it was a trick. But if not – *it was Donald Gordon*!

Meanwhile, XChiang was being assisted to a bedchamber. He was shaking and sweating. Lin So laid him down and prepared a potion to aid his master's recovery. Lin So had seen him ill before, but this was different. XChiang even appeared to be afraid. Lin So remembered what his master had said about there being someone more powerful than he. The computer hacker, Lin So was thinking. Could this be the one XChiang was referring to?

Chapter Fourteen

Djumbola climbed the hill and sat on a boulder close to the edge of a gorge. The cool morning breeze softly brushed his face and hair. His scars were not so fierce and prominent. He was totally relaxed now. Djumbola needed to empty all cares and concerns from his entire system if he was going to connect with the *all*. The future is not to see, as the saying goes. But it can be influenced. And Djumbola had done this on occasions. He just hoped that he would be allowed a further dabble. His hopes on rescuing Nefaurau depended on this. But he knew the magic would not be influenced by this fact alone. No. A lot of other considerations had to be met and satisfied. But Djumbola was in a healthy position of being highly trusted within *all* for his wisdom and truth.

He sat perfectly still. His mind was only on one subject: his son. A while elapsed, as Djumbola knew it would. It would take time for the connection and reply. It came in the form of a little bird, which flew past his seated position and perched itself on a branch of a tree nearby. A robin redbreast. It began to sing with its usual melodic tone. Soon another appeared in an adjacent tree answering the call of the first. This reminded him of the time long ago in his childhood when he had discovered a robin dying on a pathway after being attacked by a cat. Djumbola had gathered up the bird into his hands and stroked it whilst it slipped into an eternal sleep. Djumbola had turned on the cat, scolding it for killing another creature just to satisfy an urge to play. 'Only through necessity do you kill! When your life is endangered or for a meal to stave off starvation.'

He had buried the robin in a copse. Forever after this, not just robins but numerous other birds would pop out from trees and undergrowth to apparently acknowledge this past act of goodness. In fact, it was not just restricted to birds. All kinds of creatures grew to trust and respect him, as the earlier scene in the hut had attested. Others of his line would often joke, Good job Noah was not Djumbola! For he would need twenty Arks!

Both robins now trilled together. Djumbola received the message and what he had to do in repayment. He nodded his understanding and the robins both disappeared at once, leaving a very eerie silence. But Djumbola did not notice this. He had the information he required. Now it just needed a plan of action, with no more mistakes.

XChiang awoke feeling decidedly better. The potion given him by Lin So had worked wonders. His assistant was close by with tears in his eyes – of relief for his master's recovery.

'Come to me, my little rose petal,' XChiang said softly.

Lin So did so, and their lovemaking took up another hour of that day.

A polite cough disturbed their slumbers. Disentangling himself, Lin So was up on his feet in defensive mode: arms out and ready to strike. XChiang just groaned, having slightly outperformed his capacity, not yet being fully recovered from his bout of sickness.

'What is it, Li Hong?' Lin So's arms dropped to his sides as he recognised the frame behind the silk curtain surrounding the bedchamber.

Li Hong was a former Chinese wrestling champion of immense size. Unmistakable in profile. He coughed an apology. 'Forgive my intrusion, Master. But someone has arrived who I believe you have been waiting to meet.'

It was XChiang's turn to leap off the bed. He exclaimed, '*The boy. You have the boy, Nefaurau?*' He suddenly sat down again, his head swirling from an effort again too far!

Lin So chided him. 'Master, please be remembering my potions are very good but need a little more time for the after-effects to wear off.'

'Yes, yes. I hear you, Lin So. Please do not fuss. Bring the boy here, please.'

Li Hong bowed and made his departure.

XChiang was delighted that the raid had been successful. He was now back in a very strong position to bargain – to broker a deal amongst them all. Lin So, however, was still looking at him with a disapproving eye. XChiang noticed this but ignored him.

Their attention was drawn to a small boy standing before the pair. Surrounded by his captors, XChiang's personal guard. The ghost squad.

'Welcome, Nefaurau. Son of the elegant whore Sahariah, and that shameless coward, Djumbola.' XChiang was back to his formidable worst. Lin So again was shaking his head. This was no way to address someone this important from the other line. Even if he is just a boy. But Lin So had the good sense not to voice his thoughts out loud.

Nefaurau stood his ground with a steely glare at his parent's detractor. 'You are I presume the Oriental they call XChiang: the villain I have always wished to meet, so I would be able to spit the truth back at his face of what a lying, cowardly, insignificant male whore he is. There, it is said.'

XChiang's face grew dark with fury. He made as if to attack Nefaurau, but Lin So at the same time darted between the two. XChiang hesitated. Then the fist he was intending to strike Nefaurau with turned back into a flat hand. He tapped it on top of the boy's head – much to the relief of Lin So.

'Come, boy. My master is in need of more rest. I will attend to you in the meantime.'

Lin So ushered the group out then put an arm around Nefaurau and guided him also from the room, glaring with much disapproval back at XChiang. He just sniffed and lay down on the bed. Nefaurau surprisingly felt a little reassured by Lin So's reaction. He certainly did not put up any resistance, being now very relieved to have been taken out of XChiang's sight.

'Little boy, I know you are of noble descent, but a word to the wise. Please never – I mean *never* – speak to my master in those terms again. I may have saved you on this occasion, but I cannot guarantee your future safety without your strict compliance. Will you please promise me that much?'

Nefaurau looked up at the Chinaman with a strange sense of sharing common ground, a sense that this person was not in the right camp. He laughed inwardly at that involuntary thought. *Camp*! But something was niggling at him about Lin So. He shrugged it off. 'I am indebted to your kindness and wise advice. I will give your request serious consideration.'

Lin So looked up in the air, muttering, 'Please save me from the minds of those on high!' Nefaurau, understanding and appreciating his exclamation, grinned up at him, and Lin So smiled back.

The call that Steinburg was dreading most of all finally came. Not from the specialists, who were still trying to break the codes into the system, but from Weinstack. He was not a happy man.

'Jesus Christ, Steinburg. Do you know what I have just been told by one of my banks? Their whole fucking system has gone down the Swannee. Been attacked by some fucking bug, so fucking powerful it's gobbled up their back-ups as well. Nothing they can do about it they say without discovering its fucking source. And we know where that fucking source is, don't we, Steinburg? At your fucking incompetent end!'

'We are trying our best, sir. The person who carried out this sabotage obviously knew what he was doing. We think we know who it was now. A Donald Gordon. We need to trace him and get him under interrogation fast.'

'Don Gordon? I have heard that name many times. Isn't he one of the fucks who addressed us at a recent Masonic function? Fucking black motherfucker. Do you have any idea where he is?'

'We are busting a gut at this end to try and track him down. He has some damned cheek on top of all this. He actually returned to watch how things were going, skulking in the shadows. Unfortunately, our security were unaware of him being the culprit until he had left the building again.'

'Seems none of you know what you're fucking at. This could be costing me a fortune! While you lot play fucking Sherlock fucking Holmes, my assets are being well and truly fucking squeezed out of existence. My bank now says I have to provide statements, receipts, proof of fucking this and proof of fucking that. Most of that money ain't fucking clean. Here I have built up a wall of secrecy around myself, and your fucking shower is managing to dismantle it brick by fucking brick overnight!'

Steinburg found he had nothing he could say other than an apology.

'I don't want apologies, Steinburg. I want you to tell me my fucking money is safe. Get that fucking Chink to reassure me he will make good all my losses. After all, it's his fucking system that is fucking everything up. When's this meeting?'

'I will get back to XChiang and let you know as soon as I have a time for it.' Steinburg waited for another rant but the line just disconnected.

When XChiang woke again, he asked Lin So to prepare the secret room for a ceremony. Thousands of years had passed, but one simple ceremony survived through his family traditions. It was also an incantation to one powerful source, whose assistance he needed now more than ever. One simple act could move a mountain.

After the ceremony, XChiang received a call from his special advisors... on the most secure of lines. 'Mr XChiang, we are extremely sorry to hear of the problems you are experiencing. It transpires that Donald Gordon aka Djumbola is responsible for the catastrophic events of the loss of your systems. It, unfortunately, gets worse. Having destroyed your system, the virus appears to be now following connections into other areas. A general alert has been put out but this cannot be fully effective until we can access the main culprit and destroy it.'

XChiang listened silently to this information. As he had predicted, one stronger was now matched against him. He should be feeling afraid but the ceremony had refreshed his purpose. He felt strength anew. 'This Djumbola – have you any way of detecting his presence?'

'Unfortunately not, Mr XChiang. He is as elusive as he is competent in reeking havoc. Not so one George Coney. Are you aware of this incompetent and how much his foolishness and neglect played a part in Gordon being able to access the system?'

'I am, thank you. But I understand he has been spirited away within the confines of Masonic mystery?'

'That is also our understanding. Very poetic, if I might say so, Mr XChiang: Masonic mystery. But it is no mystery who are also after him. A magazine was discovered with the file. Gordon posted it to a contact on an Indian Reservation. It featured modern day scalping of Native Americans and the sale of the hair to a perverted readership. Can you imagine how those Native Americans are taking it? I have reliable information that Coney will be found very soon hanging from his own hair!'

'Very interesting. Even amusing, despite the circumstances. But I thought he was bald?'

'Depends where on his body they are going to suspend him from. How much weight can pubic hair take before it starts to pull out?' There was a short chuckle.

XChiang was also laughing. 'Ouch! Remind me not to upset Native Americans ever.' There were mutual bouts of laughter at both ends of the line.

'Getting back to business, Mr Xchiang, we believe you may have been further compromised. Someone else in your employ. The gap which opened up to allow Nefaurau through has been plugged again. The information of the whereabouts of this hole could only have come from one of your party. At the same time, they discovered our mole within their line – a tremendous blow to all of our efforts.'

XChiang was no longer laughing. This information had hit him like a sledgehammer. Someone in his employ? Someone who knew where the hole was. A ghost guard… surely not! He suddenly froze, remembering something else. The instigator of this latest coup of securing Nefaurau: Lin So. The sudden realisation caused his heart to begin weeping blood!

At the other end of the line there was detection from the silence that this was not good news for XChiang's ears. He had obviously taken it badly: the fact that a close member of his trusted entourage was a spy. But it was also known to those on the other end of the line who this was. But he had to affect a degree of sangfroid to keep matters smooth as could possibly be under such trying circumstances. Still consummate professionals – on both ends of the line!

'Thank you again for your diligence. The usual fee plus an extra large bonus to be forwarded. I hasten to add I will await the conclusion of the parasite's movement in the banking system before I send such monies. I hope this will meet with your approval.'

'Mr XChiang, as always it is a privilege and a pleasure to be dealing on your behalf. We fully agree with your assessment. We also hope that matters work out favourably for you. We will remain vigilant at our end.'

'Thank you for your continued support, gentlemen. I must now take my leave.' He disconnected the line. 'They knew who it was too. But were gracious enough at least not to put *that* in my face as well.' He burst into tears. A combination of anger, frustration and sadness over a lost love.

The meeting had been arranged at a villa on a remote island off the coast of mainland Greece. Half the attendees were major players in the group. The rest, including Steinburg, were subordinates – gofers for the rest! But every person, despite the differences in status had, given the gravity of the situation, been ferried in, after private jets had linked them to the nearest airports. All received equal transportation rights on this special occasion. The remainder of the group were attached to secure video links, including Henry Weinstack.

The assembly was becoming noisy, with heated debates going on between many of them, amid a general air of disenchantment. XChiang had been dealing with the other matters. Now, from just outside the room, he was listening to the throng, not really learning anything new. Vultures the lot of them. But what do vultures do if the pickings dry up? Would they turn on each other? Well, they were making a good show of that at present.

The door to the room opened. The noise suddenly died down, the hubbub receded. All eyes were now on the entrance of an immaculately dressed XChiang in the full flowing robes of an ancient past dynasty. He looked at each of the group in turn. His burning stare left no one in doubt. This meeting was on XChiang's terms – and it wasn't going to be a party!

There's always someone, however, who misses the point. 'What the fuck is going on, XChiang? I have had to leave a very important meeting of creditors to fly to this godforsaken island at a moment's notice. Now I learn the world's banking system is failing. For fuck's sake, XChiang, what is going on? Is this another of your exotic whims?'

There was general laughter at this. The speaker milked it for all it was worth and continued. 'We lesser mortals have to earn a living. We can't earn it whilst eating a Chinese!' The laughter in some quarters was now hoarse.

On his initial sweep of the room XChiang had taken in the various expressions: those who were here for a fight, but only if backed up by others; and those who were already strong enough in their own right to disturb proceedings. He reckoned that the first section were a million miles away from the two or three main players. And they would only stick together if the goo was that thick!

Inscrutable as ever on such occasions, XChiang trained his sight on the figure who was voicing his complaint. The rest of the ensemble noticing XChiang's view directed their gaze also in this direction.

George Henry *Lloyd's* predecessors had made fortunes from outwitting investors with a scheme purporting to be able to make each of them rich by investing in what had been falsely reported as a great find in some gold mines in New Guinea. This being an island inhabited by head hunters at the time meant there weren't many private investigators who were willing to risk their necks, literally, for a cause of establishing the truth of the matter. But human nature being as it is, many investors did take the risk and invested large amounts in the project. They signed legal papers which were later to prove worthless as the Lloyds disappeared with their money, only to resurface a few years later as a respectable financial consultancy. What was not lost on the creditors was the fact of George's grandfather's high position within Masonic circles.

'May I welcome you, each and every one, in these trying times for us all. Mr Lloyd, I have listened to your rhetoric. Knowing your own particular family history of depriving clients of their ill-gotten gains, I must admit to finding a certain amount of irony with the fact I have brought you away from such a meeting of creditors. Maybe, the full circle of probabilities is now falling within your lap, my friend.'

Lloyd was about to reply but noticed XChiang holding a hand

up to stop him. 'Someone in this room has compromised the whole operation. His idiot aide has done for us all.' XChiang waited for the reaction. He was directing his stare at Steinburg.

Steinburg reacted. 'What are you on about now, XChiang? Changing the rules to suit yourself?'

'Mr Steinburg, you yourself are here to answer why we have this problem in the first place.' XChiang's eyes were now on Weinstack.

Steinburg was now extremely agitated. He directed it at the nearest available source: Luis *Rodrigues* – a Latino gofer extraordinaire. In Steinburg's terms, another foreign faggot who was beneath contempt.

'Well, Rodrigues? Can't fucking blame you really. You're not close enough to the rest to know – I mean fucking *know*. What is going on now is a power overthrow. This fucking Chink wants to take over the whole show. All the fucking work everyone has put into it. Do any of you trust this motherfucker? Because if you do – not just you Rodrigues – all of you are well and truly fucked. He has had previous dealings. All of his lot have. As long as you can count backwards, his fucking clan of yellow-assed fuckers have been at it. Cut him fucking loose. He is one sorry-assed fucking ultimate fucking loser. He has trusted his own kind all through this – and even that he can't get fucking right.'

The last sentence stung XChiang. It was moments old in terms of fact but how this nonentity knew could be a future problem. XChiang made a mental note to set someone out to discover this source! The room had fallen silent. Most of those there had acknowledged Steinburg's impertinence.

Lin So appeared in the full dress of a Manchurian courtesan.

'Fucking faggot!' was the greeting he received from the Steinburg corner.

XChiang did not look at his assistant but glared at the now prone heap in a chair which was Steinburg. 'Mr Steinburg, forgive me. But is not a faggot to be found in your own terminology "up its own ass", but at the same time still searching for the reason someone else might want to enter the same shit-hole as well?'

Those in the room delayed reaction to this. But a snigger somewhere ended up with guffaws elsewhere.

'Eh? XChiang, what the fuck are you on about?' Steinburg did not even have the courtesy to look at XChiang as he spoke. Instead he opened a case and began rummaging around.

Suddenly the room was circled by a host of devil-masked entities. All were dressed similarly in old oriental garments. A knife had penetrated Steinburg's hand, pinning it to the case. He cried out in pain but looked up in horror as another of the team held a sword to his neck.

The rest of the congregation were gasping sounds of utter disbelief. Some others were about to sever connection, including Weinstack.

But XChiang got in first. 'Any – I mean *any* – of you leave this meeting before I conclude will be considered in breach of our conditions. And you know what that will mean. Also, I will take it personally as a hostile act against my personal liberty.'

XChiang waited a short time for the room to settle. All appeared to be paying attention. However, Steinburg was shaking like a leaf.

'You want an explanation?' XChiang looked at each in return. Some half nodded. Others, including Weinstack, looked blank.

'Whatever. A George Coney. Ring any bells with you?' XChiang waited for a reaction. Some murmured indistinct replies; Steinburg was amongst them.

'I am sorry, Mr Steinburg. I did not quite get that.' XChiang's eye was piercing but not as uncomfortable as the weapon at Steinburg's neck. He was going to make some form of reply, but then thought better of it. He looked defeated.

'Well, for any of you who do not know of this cretin, George Coney, I will elucidate. He is in fact one of you Westerners who believe joining secret societies is the way to enlightenment. That security in another heaven. Maybe that is possible. Who knows? But I truly believe at this very moment in time George Coney is meeting with his rightful end. Maybe he wasn't that clever. Maybe he was acting under orders. Maybe some of you wish to rid this group of anyone that does not fit your colour scheme and ride off into a sunset like in your old cowboy films. You have had your own ways for too long, disappearing anyone who offends your white sensitivities. You carry on believing you will inherit some kind of heaven, but this is never going to happen for you Manifest Destiny types.'

'Jesus protect me! What are you saying? Many of my South Americano compatriots are still *the missing*. They disappeared. All the other countries surrounding us have similar tales to tell. Are you saying all this is a conspiracy backed up by whites against all other non-whites? Why? We are poor and basically inoffensive people. But poor people in bad lands are obviously in the way of some kind of progress – hasn't it always been that way? I certainly can see that now.'

Steinburg was the first to react. 'Rodrigues, for fuck's sake shut your stupid spic mouth. How far do we go back? Trust me, this Chink is just stirring things up for his own ends.'

Rodrigues made no eye contact with Steinburg as if this would lead to further contamination.

'Well, fuck you, Rodrigues. And fuck the rest of you if there is another war!' Steinburg strained against the blade in order to look across at the video link to Weinstack, who was looking down at his desk.

'Mr Weinstack, thank you for your tolerance so far in such trying circumstances, and for your attending this meeting. It is a pity you could not make it in person.' XChiang gave him a slight bow.

Weinstack looked up, glaring back at XChiang. 'Let's get one thing straight, XChiang. I don't like being patronised. Especially by some slant-eyed fucker who I wouldn't even employ to wipe the dog shit off my shoes. Another thing. If I were there, would I also be carrying a fucking sword blade on my neck? How can you expect to be trusted when you throw your weight around like that? Get that fucking sword off Nelson Ho and attend to his hand wound. XChiang stop behaving like an ancient moronic Chink boss and get in the real fucking world. And you, Nelson Ho, if you know what is good for you, you will shut that fat trap of yours up. Do you understand, Steinburg?'

Steinburg nodded to the screen, but Weinstack was still glaring at XChiang, waiting for him to give an order to his men. XChiang took this opportunity to glance at Lin So. 'What would you advise me to do, trusted and faithful servant?'

Lin So was a little surprised at the formality of his master's words. He glanced back with a quizzing look, but XChiang gave nothing else away.

'Well, Lin So?'

'I do not wish to offend you, Master. But I would consider it a grave mistake to harm Mr Steinburg any further. I realise he has insulted your hospitality and made terrible accusations, but I sense others will be dealing with him.' Lin So looked down purposely in deference to XChiang.

'Thank you, Lin So. I thought you might say exactly that. As always you seem to know what is best. So I will follow your advice one more time.'

Lin So again felt the strangeness in his Master. What is he really thinking? Is he really reaching the edge this time? Or has he something else up that flowing sleeve of his?

XChiang waved a hand to his guards. The sword was removed from Steinburg's neck and the dagger was unceremoniously yanked up from the case at the same time, exiting from the back of his hand. Blood poured from the gaping wound. Another attendant rushed forward and tended to this, wrapping a bandage tightly around the dressing. Steinburg still shook throughout this process. Being in shock, he actually thanked the attendant for his assistance, much to XChiang's amusement.

'So what are you going to do next, XChiang? There must be some smart-assed Chinese proverb covering this situation of your making.' Despite the gravity of the meeting there were sounds of quiet laughter at Weinstack's remark.

'Mr Weinstack, again I am humbled by your astute awareness of my brilliance. My judgement has always been considered sound, obviously with the assistance of my close and wise attendants. But my senses are thousands of years old, backed up by dynasties you Americans can only dream about. Tell me, Mr Weinstack, if you could exchange your bigotry on all matters Oriental at this very moment – maybe throw in a billion or three – which, on reflection, you might not possibly be good for anyway at the present time... do you think there would be any takers amongst my family? If you think for a minute that could ever be brokered, Mr Weinstack, then all I can say is you really underestimate us. But I think you Westerners have been underestimating us in the Far East for far too long.'

'Nice speech, XChiang. Pity it was full of crap.' Weinstack raised a further bout of laughter.

'Well, back to the business at hand. I'm not referring to *your* hand, Mr Steinburg. I do hope it makes a rapid recovery so you are able to use it again soon.'

Steinburg glared at XChiang. 'Always taking the piss, aren't you? I think sometime someone is going to catch up with you and give you the fucking kicking you deserve.'

Weinstack coughed. 'Nelson Ho, What did I tell you? Stop insulting the natives. This dragon slayer has some pretty potent magic up his sleeve. Haven't you, XChiang?'

'Thank you again for your compliment, Mr Weinstack. I do indeed have magical powers. Perhaps we will be witnessing some in the very near future.' XChiang beamed with delight.

'Like can you make yourself disappear? Like forever? That would be a neat trick!' Steinburg immediately realised what he had said and glanced across at the vi-link, nodding an apology to Weinstack.

An attendant entered the room and handed a note to Lin So, who quickly read it. Then he handed it to XChiang.

'Gentlemen, I have confirmation here that most of the networks affected by our virus have managed to stall it and are now in the process of containing it sufficiently to be able to get back to some kind of normality. We are warned that severe disruption to all services has been experienced, and in many cases whole systems of information have been wiped out – including back-ups. Only time will tell just how seriously our own web has been damaged.'

Weinstack had been taking an incoming call whilst XChiang had been reporting the news. 'XChiang, I heard some of that, enough to realise we are in a fucking mess. That call was to reaffirm my earlier fears of my accounts being lost in this turmoil. No trace can be found of assets stretching into billions. I hope you are good for this, XChiang – and for the rest of our group, who will all be in the same fucking boat. Most of us depended entirely on wiring our funds to and fro, keeping it on the move to evade the fucking taxman and all the other leeching spies. But now most of this probably will never resurface, unless we are extremely lucky. And just now I don't think any of us feel like betting our last two cents on anything you are riding, XChiang!' There were murmurs of agreement all around the room.

XChiang again addressed the assembly. 'Gentlemen, gentlemen! If I can have your attention again. Whatever position you are finding yourselves in, think of this. The person who destroyed our system and damaged our web was masquerading as a Donald Gordon. Working in the same unit as George Coney.'

'So have we found this fucker yet?' Weinstack asked. 'Can we buy him? Will he give us the file back if the price is right?'

Steinburg agreed. 'Yeah, yeah. So this fucker has messed us. What's his price? Everyone has his price. Coney fucked up. We all agree on that. So, okay, this guy might be in it for a pay-off.'

Weinstack was glaring at Steinburg with a look telling him again to button it. Steinburg held his hands out to him and shrugged another apology.

'Tut, tut, Mr Steinburg. And you, Mr Weinstack. You both live in a completely different world to me. How many billions are you willing to offer up for the cause?'

This again struck Weinstack like a slap in the face. Given his dire financial prospects, he was not happy at XChiang's obviously loaded remark. 'Fuck off, Xchiang!'

George Lloyd now butted in. 'I see nothing wrong in an arrangement like that. Would this Gordon chap accept a monetary persuasion?'

XChiang shook his head, looking down. 'Gentlemen, Donald Gordon has been confirmed to me as Djumbola. An ancient priest. I have already mentioned he cannot be persuaded. That is a mild observation. A general insight into this person would take a long time to describe. However, I will not waste your time in this respect. The simple fact is, this man's soul is incorruptible.'

'Impossible! Everyone has a price eventually. You just have not approached this Gordon guy in the correct manner! Give me an hour with him and I will persuade the son of a bitch. Then we can ambush him afterwards. Once he has the money he will drop his guard. People always do in those situations.'

All in the room appeared to agree with this latest Weinstack idea, apart from XChiang, who was now visibly becoming tired of how the proceedings were heading.

He raised his hands again to quieten the throng. 'Donald Gordon is Djumbola who is Donald Gordon. The two are the same entity. Djumbola is from a dynasty as old as my own. Very few weaknesses, if any at all. A worthy adversary. I sense we will be meeting him soon. Then we can discuss it all with him. And you who believe he can be bought will have ample opportunity to test your theory.'

Weinstack stood up, knocking over his chair at the same time. 'Well if he can't be bought, nail the fucker to a cross – like was done to that other sad incorruptible bastard.'

'Mr Weinstack, please remember, even though it is far from my own religion, there are Christians amongst the rest of this group.' XChiang's tongue was almost protruding through his amazing cheek! 'But is that an admission of guilt?'

For a moment Weinstack looked confused. Then the penny dropped. 'Ha fucking ha, XChiang. Bit outside my time, huh?'

XChiang wandered over closer to the vi-link, bending down so that his face was close to the screen and he looked fully into Weinstack's beady eyes. 'Who knows? I think it is still a possibility. I mean, your bigotry must have commenced very early on for you to have reached the level you are at now!'

Weinstack's face went purple with rage. 'You cheeky, patronising, rice-eating, ass-fucking, cock-sucking, slant-eyed, motherfucking Chink! You're not worth a wok!'

'Not guilty to some of those accusations. But guilty to the rest, Your Honour!' The room was alive again with laughter – at the expense of both of them.

'Alright, you ask me what I can do for you all? You, Mr Weinstack, mentioned my prowess in all things magical. These powers have served me well enough through thousands of years. I know many of you will scoff at such a statement, not believing our souls can keep returning to this accursed earth again and again. But in that ignorance, so much is lost on your own souls and treated as gains by those who would seek to dupe you into believing as you do. I have the power to transport each and every one of you to a place where you will experience safety and comfort. But this is not the place you consider has been promised you elsewhere, a place for you all to take your vast fortunes. That's a myth, gentlemen. Your personal fortunes must stay here in this world. To fund the back-up required until the time is right.'

'You seriously want us to believe all that bullshit? Leave our fortunes in your hands? Is this what all the fucking system failure nonsense is about? You had all the codes. So this could all be a massive scam to bleed us dry anyways.' Weinstack had the room roaring again.

XChiang stood looking down, shaking his head. He waited for the commotion to die down again. 'I will remind you, gentlemen. The mighty rock is just a shade away from this world. None of my powers can alter its course. As it nears, more funds than ever will be required to finance your security. There will be undoubted widespread panic… mass demonstrations over the lack of planning for the rest of the populace… anarchy. Security will be the key to all. It will have to combat the worsening situation. Thus funding is imperative. Once the asteroid has completed its mission, we will then see if earth is still habitable. Anything would be possible for us if it were. I leave it to you, gentlemen, to decide. Right now, I need a break. Refreshments will be served. I will return soon – with a surprise.'

Just outside of sight and hearing of those at the meeting stood a party who was very interested in the course of events, listening intently to all. He knew well what surprise XChiang had in store for his guests; but the surprises would not end there. For Djumbola had arrived now for his son, Nefaurau.

Chapter Fifteen

Those actually at the meeting were still chatting quietly amongst themselves when XChiang returned. Weinstack, still on vi-link, saw the entrance and shouted, 'Hey, you fucking tight-assed Chink! Where's my refreshments?' The room resounded again to sounds of laughter.

XChiang was becoming tired of Weinstack's little game of insults. 'Mr Weinstack?'

'Yes? *Chinkie noodle went to town riding on a dumb ass, put a feather up his crack and called it Hong Kong poo, eh!*'

The room now erupted at Weinstack's rendition sung to the old song with his new lyrics.

'Mr Weinstack?' XChiang again asked patiently.

'Well, what now, XChiang?' Weinstack replied whilst still milking the applause.

'Do you feel something sharp on your bulbous neck?'

'Eh? What the fuck—!'

Clearly on the screen could be seen the edge of a sword blade pressing down on Weinstack's neck. The room immediately hushed. Silent gasps of astonishment could be heard.

'Mr Weinstack, if it were refreshments you really required they would have been served you. But as you can see, your actions and words have provoked a fury in my guard of attendants, who would clearly be delighted with my order for your head to be removed from your revolting body.'

'Fuck you, XChiang!' Weinstack managed before the sword was pushed further into his neck. Tiny droplets of blood began to drip to the floor.

'And for the rest of you on vi-link, please be assured you have also members of my elite guard waiting in the wings. Now, if there are no further interruptions, I will proceed.'

XChiang waved a hand to the waiting Lin So, who in turn ushered in the procession. XChiang was grinning now in triumph. All eyes were on the entrance of a small boy surrounded by his own special guard of XChiang's ninja warriors.

'This is Nefaurau, son of Sahariah, Priestess of all. And Djumbola who you have already heard about.'

Nefaurau, although obviously extremely frightened, glared at XChiang. He summoned all his nerve and faced XChiang. '*You*. You are responsible for the terrible things happening in this world. My mother has informed me of the facts. Many thought my father was to blame. But it was you… I have come to tell you to your face. I am not afraid of you, XChiang.'

XChiang's expression changed. He growled. 'You are in no position to speak to me of fear. You have no idea what I may have saved up for you. A special delight for my hungry warriors!' XChiang laughed manically, causing Lin So to wince.

Nefaurau was still unbowed. 'Do as you please, XChiang. Whatever orifice pleases you and your kind. But you can never enter my soul. And it will forever hunt you down. As for this rabble, you are just showing off to them. But I do not believe you could possibly win them over. They cannot be that stupid. The slaying of a priest of nature is forbidden, XChiang. You knew this. But there, you are already showing the first signs of madness attached to such a deed. Your blood is cursed!'

XChiang stood back from the child, snatching a sword from a guard. He then advanced towards Nefaurau, who stood his ground. XChiang's eye began to quiver as he glared at the boy. Nefaurau returned the stare, but he was weakening. XChiang held the sword up ready to strike. In that moment, Lin So rushed forward and held XChiang's arm aloft. XChiang's eyes now swelled to manic proportions. He shrugged Lin So off and began again to strike at Nefaurau… but he could not move. It felt like he had been encased in cement.

A voice spoke from the darkened space in the corner of the room. 'For as long as I have known you, XChiang, you have always lacked something. A lack of humility plays havoc with your temperament. Picking on a child: add that to the list. It's not looking good for you.'

Djumbola walked over to the prone figure and wrenched the sword from XChiang's extended hand. Then he took Nefaurau's hand and walked him to Lin So. Turning on his heel, he made a circuit of the room wrenching swords from all the armed guards – who, like XChiang, were in the attitude of attack when they were made motionless. A tear ran down the face of Nefaurau. Lin So saw it, and hugged the boy close.

The rest of those in the room were staring now in absolute dread at the spectacle. Suddenly XChiang and his army were in motion again, bewildered; looking closely about them for their missing weapons. XChiang glared first at the sight of Lin So protecting the child, then at his adversary, with a loathing, withering stare. His contempt for Djumbola was now at an all-time high! But he kept an inscrutable smile on his face, a mask of politeness.

'But of course, Djumbola, has not your own head rested on stones whilst the remainder of your carcass fell elsewhere? Do you remember those times?'

Djumbola smiled an equally inscrutable one back at him. 'Of course, I remember well enough. Your family of thieves and vagabonds have always treated me with the utmost disrespect!' He feigned a slight bow of allegiance to the Chinaman.

'The magic appears to be with you, Djumbola. But I know it too. All here have worked very hard for their place in the sun. It will not be easy for you to convince them they must give it all up. We wish for you to release the grip you have over us. For this you may have your child back. If not, I have many ways of dealing with him. I promise you, only the cleanest of penises will be allowed to enter Nefaurau.'

Djumbola's face clouded for a moment. 'Hell hath no fury, XChiang.'

'A woman… ha ha! All women are only fit for use as concubines. Either in the harem or brothel – if there's a difference!' XChiang again laughed manically.

'Even your mother, sister and grandmother, XChiang?'

'No exceptions. This is a man's world, Djumbola!' XChiang's face mask was taking on demonic proportions.

'Perhaps it is more a fact that women will not allow men into their own.' Djumbola's eyes glinted as he spoke.

XChiang snorted. 'If you believe that you will believe anything.'

'It is interesting to discover the depth of your lack of philosophy, XChiang. But of course maybe you are the cause of prostitution being the oldest of professions. As with all women-haters, your kind have made this world just so. Many of you still prefer other ways of gratification. The dreaded sodomites. Preferring to mate with anything other than what nature intended. And most cowardly of all, hiding behind those who are branded as performing deeds against nature but who would never consider harming nature itself. These have no truck with women. They in fact love women for their existence. But your kind – this is where the pure hatred originates from. But there we are; your kind's disrespect of nature is why you are being punished without even realising it.' Djumbola's stare was now beginning to discomfort XChiang as much as his words. His expression slipped for a moment. He glared back at Djumbola, who was now expecting XChiang to pounce. But the Chinaman composed himself again.

'You wish me to relax my grip on your little group in exchange for the boy? I do not find this a problem.'

XChiang looked puzzled. 'What trickery are you planning now, Djumbola? You cede too easily.'

'You have me at a disadvantage, XChiang. I have been fortunate with power over you up till now. But, as you appreciate yourself, one little slip and my son would be at your mercy. Sahariah would never forgive me if I allowed Nefaurau to be further harmed. But having said that, XChiang, it is not my grip on your kind which should be of concern to you. Believe me, you have already upset a greater magic than mine. It will pursue you for all time. I have its promise on that!'

XChiang tried hard not to let his mask slip, but momentarily his eyes portrayed fear. 'You mean Sahariah?' He looked over at Nefaurau, who whilst still afraid managed a defiant stare in return. Djumbola felt immense pride for his son. He waited for XChiang's attention to be returned to himself.

'Nature, XChiang. *Nature*. No one single entity is any more important than the whole. I might have had the grand title of High Priest once, but it was only a term to identify my purpose within nature's framework. Nature's web. Which is the reason why my slaying was forbidden, you fool. It's too late now for regrets. Your kind have created extreme wealth for the few. Brainwashing populations to accept your views on God-ordained religions, Royalty, kingdoms. And what do you give them in return? But your ignorance of natural magic has caused catastrophic misplacement inside the web. Nature *will* balance – whether by my assistance, Sahariah's, or maybe even through its own self-regulation. Do not forget the rock heading towards this planet.'

XChiang snorted derisively at Djumbola's rhetoric. 'We plan to be far gone from here when that arrives. I have promised this much: another existence far from here, where the chosen ones will be hailed as heroes for all the wisdom and knowledge we bring with us.'

'And if I release my grip, this is your aim?' Djumbola shook his head. 'But you haven't been listening have you? I can open a doorway, but what is on the other side to meet you…?'

'We are willing to take that chance.' XChiang was now swaying slightly, but without a Lin So to catch him if he were to fall.

Djumbola sensed the closeness of a power source. He knew it was now his call!

Djumbola closed his eyes. His face took on a ferocious expression, followed by calmness and serenity. This expressional change continued for some moments. He then raised both arms, producing a thin rod which he held between thumb and forefinger of his left hand. At first it lay inert, facing down. Then Djumbola began chanting. As he did so he began a dance slowly moving from one foot to the other, slowly turning in a circle. The rod began to rise, vibrating at the same time. The whole room seemed to echo this vibration. Suddenly, holes appeared on lines representing the four winds, which rushed through meeting in the centre, creating a circle which began slowly to rise towards the ceiling.

On reaching the ceiling a fifth hole appeared, opening up a vista brightly illuminated by the night-time stars and full moon. Djumbola was now in the centre of the whirlwind, slowly rising.

Suddenly, from the Northern door Sahariah and her entourage appeared, rushing through. A bolt of lightning coursed through the room, east to west, temporarily blinding all in the room. As if in slow motion, XChiang watched Sahariah grasp up her child and exit through the south door, followed closely by her attendants, who had fought off the unarmed ghost squad more easily than they could have expected. XChiang, however, had picked up a sword, which he swung, decapitating Lin So as he too rushed towards the door and safety.

XChiang then flung the weapon to the floor. The agony of losing his only love consumed him, and at the same time he realised how much Djumbola had duped him. This caused him to instinctively spring at the Blackman, through the wind into the central spiral. Djumbola feinted a move one way, then went the other, leaving XChiang clutching thin air. Stepping backwards out of the vortex, Djumbola pointed the rod forward at the spiralling wind that contained the figure of XChiang. The look on XChiang's face told its own story. He too tried to step out, only to find himself trapped in what now had turned into a mini-tornado. XChiang began to rise with the uplifting force field. With panic etched on his face, arms windmilling, legs treading thin air, he mouthed a silent scream.

Djumbola uttered a few more words of the incantation, then threw the rod into the spiral. Suddenly the winds changed direction, rushing back through the four voids, leaving the fifth wind in a form of limbo. The rod turned upwards towards the animated figure of XChiang, splitting into two parts as it rose. These pierced XChiang's underarms, lifting him further towards the gap in the ceiling. Still screaming in silent tones inside the whirlwind, XChiang looked down at his enemy. But Djumbola was ready for the impact. XChiang's intended evil eye lost its force. Djumbola returned it with a piece of his own.

As a soft boiled egg runs when fractured, so XChiang's eyes oozed, dripping a congealed mess. Then the wind tunnel suddenly disappeared through into the heavens, taking XChiang with it to his own personal hell.

The room reverted to normality. Missing from the assembly were, of course, XChiang, Nefaurau and Lin So, whose headless body had been gathered up by cloaked figures and taken through the doorway. Also gone were XChiang's private ninja army.

'Jesus fucking Christ! What was that all about?' Henry Weinstack had regained his voice, his potential assassins having departed also. The rest of the group were in shock, aghast at the events witnessed, with ashen faces. They were unable to quite understand or believe what they had seen with their own eyes, and they were afraid. Very afraid. Nobody wanted to look Djumbola in the eye!

Djumbola himself looked drained. His shoulders were hunched but his stare was still firm. He looked at each of the group, including those on vi-link. He could guess what they were thinking. He stepped back into the centre of the room so that all could see him plainly. Strangely, in hindsight, those on vi-link, excepting of course Henry Weinstack, could have severed connection during the melee. Maybe morbid curiosity had overcome their survival instinct. Or maybe they were all still frozen stiff with fear!

'I am very pleased none of you have left the meeting. As you will have noticed, XChiang will not be in a position to close the minutes of your meeting for today.'

One or two choked back laughter. But not Weinstack. 'That is all very well for you to say. You are one clever motherfucker, aren't you, Don Gordon – or fucking whoever you are. But you have fucked up some of us to such an extent that we'll be begging on the fucking streets.'

Djumbola measured a response. 'Mr Weinstack. I have always looked on you as someone who will always be there for another. Unfortunately, that other would possibly have expired before you moved even sideways in order to give life-saving assistance!' The laughter now continued.

'Well, fuck the lot of you!' Weinstack by now wanted to recoil into his secret kingdom. But Djumbola had not finished.

'Mr Weinstack, you want to ask me about the codes. Is this correct?'

Weinstack, his finger on the disconnect, hesitated. 'What the fuck does it matter anymore? I am done for.'

'Mr Weinstack, will you acknowledge you have always distanced yourself from the rest of humanity?'

Weinstack looked through his screen at his vision of Djumbola. 'What are you getting at, Blackman?'

'Mr Weinstack, I have to say you are not helping matters. You were quick enough to ram that fact down Mr Steinburg's throat. But I realise maybe XChiang was right about you. Maybe the xenophobia is that deep – that far back for you to change.'

'I am listening, Blackman. Nothing you have said so far is making sense to me.'

'Mistah Weinstack, I realise you still see my kind as slaves. But unfortunately for you, this black boy is gonna whop yer hide if you's not comin' acrawss. Yo savvy, white boy?'

Weinstack scratched his head. 'What?'

'I say once again, Mr Weinstack. And now the rest of your people are listening. You are, or should I say *were*, the dominant feature in all of this, being so rich and that. But maybe that has changed for you. You are also asking, What has this black fucker done with the file? Am I correct on that assumption?'

'Near enough. Not enough vitriol, though!' Even though he was hating this and would never admit otherwise, Weinstack was in some way warming to this upstart.

'Well said, Mr Weinstack. I promise you, if you had made any effort to beg forgiveness or offered a bribe beyond your means, I would have walked out here and now.'

Weinstack was now confused. He started to say something but realised now that maybe anything he said would be turned back at him again. He remained silent.

'Yes, I still have the file. And believe me, gentlemen, those who were in composition of it will be regretting it being in my hands. Not forgetting your much lamented leader, Hyiang XChiang – who will, at this very moment, be blindly going where he has never gone before. This will stay with me until such time I see the rest of you performing in a manner befitting the rest of mankind.'

'You know you have sufficient in that file to do for the lot of us. Why are you giving us this chance?' said Weinstack, slumped into his chair.

Rodrigues got to his feet. 'Yes. Why are you giving us this chance? You could surely obliterate us as you have XChiang.'

Djumbola nodded. 'This world still needs leaders, or everything will turn into a chaotic mess. Even I do not want such a catastrophe, partly caused by my wiping you out of the picture. I just hope you have learned some kind of lesson now. That some goodness can come out of some of you. For some, I do not suppose that is possible overnight. Or even many overnights.' Djumbola made a point of glaring at Weinstack and then Steinburg. Both were for once speechless. 'There are a lot of decent folk out there who deserve better from the higher authorities of this planet. Before you are all hit by the rock.'

'You mean it's really going to happen?' Rodrigues said. 'The asteroid we keep hearing about? But we also hear that it will be dealt with by the scientists and the military.'

'You put too much faith into such stories. You trust your scientists to always come up with a solution and for your armies always to have sufficient firepower to blow away any ole enemy. Not this time, buddy. Put it this way: you have just as much chance as any of those Japanese schoolchildren had of blowing away with bubble sticks the bombs which fell on their Hiroshima and Nagasaki. I do not believe anyone who supported such action has any comprehension of how angry that made the ones who really matter. Nature has a way of returning the compliment.'

'But those fucking Japs deserved it! They were committing atrocities and would not surrender. It had to be done,' Weinstack shouted through his link-up.

'So I understand. But what if say the Native American population had strung up such devices and bombed some of your cities? Were not the same kind of atrocities visited on these peoples in your country's march of progress under the flag of Manifest Destiny? The Japanese, as with many other tribes, were only really guilty of naivety, more than anything else. What excuse have so-called civilised regimes to offer for their kind of barbarity in the name of liberty? I tell you, gentlemen – Manifest Destiny?

The rock comes to remind all that nature, and only nature, decides destiny.'

Rodrigues looked despairingly at Djumbola. 'Is this the honest truth?' Djumbola nodded. 'Then we are in a hell of a mess. I don't know about the rest of you, but I would consider it an honour to work for you if you would stay and help us through our troubles. Perhaps even you could be the new leader?'

Most of the others present appeared to be in agreement with this proposal.

'Gentlemen. I am extremely flattered at your invitation, but I must decline. I have already stretched beyond my natural parameters. You must find the strength and goodness to change sufficiently and combat this problem yourselves. With XChiang out of your way, you at least have a chance. He is sitting somewhere I prepared for him, without doubt feeling very sorry for himself. For he has his blindness now to go with all the other failings.'

'You mean he is still alive?' Weinstack was incredulous.

'Yes, Mr Weinstack. But he will be wishing he wasn't! I have prepared many trials for him to undergo. He will never leave that place. Only I can rescind the spell around him. And I have no intention of ever doing that, my friend.' Djumbola looked into Weinstack's eyes. He got the message loud and clear. Weinstack visibly gulped.

'One aspect however, where XChiang was correct. I cannot be bought. His nightmare became reality because of that simple fact. This world has a structure of values and beliefs which is assessed and policed by unnatural forces. The corrupt are valued over the incorruptible. Money is truly the root of all your problems here. But you have made it into a monster which you thought you could control. Greed cannot be controlled! Until you can change this in human nature you will never succeed.'

This struck a chord with George Lloyd. 'Well, Mr Weinstack, you said to give you an hour with him and you would be able to change his mind. Still hold to that?'

Weinstack made no reply. He just snorted and swung his chair around so his back was to the screen. This caused a ripple of muted laughter.

Djumbola continued his point. 'Wave all your wealth in the face of anything on this earth which is not human. See it dance to your tune because of it, and I promise you I will join XChiang in his sightless kingdom and copulate with him until the stars fall. Is my point clear?' More laughter at Weinstack's expense.

'I must take my leave of you now… tiring day and all that. I wish you good fortune with your efforts. I will be watching from near or afar.' Djumbola once again swept an eye across his audience. Then he stepped backwards and disappeared.

Chapter Sixteen

Cal and Sara were debating what to do next. Should they stay there in the hut until Djumbola returned, or make a break for it and take their chances? A moment later their wishes came true.

They found themselves at the apartment rented by Cal. It took a while to tidy up, but nothing major. In fact, it appeared that those who had invaded Cal's space had been themselves the subject of some kind of disturbance which had made them depart early. There was a ring of E about the place. Not ecstasy, but his brother! Lots of hot wiring set up before his demise, there to dissuade intruders. Several had been tripped giving out nasty shocks and at the same time triggering alarms directly linked to the police. Cal wondered at this, trying to imagine the scene.

Both were extremely tired but neither wished for bed and sleep. Something was bothering the pair of them. Cal turned on the television, flicking through the channels with the remote. Nothing grabbed their attention. Sara decided to flop on the sofa bed. Against her better judgement, she dozed off. Cal had the sound right down low on the television, listening to her quiet snores. But he suddenly leapt up on seeing familiar faces on the screen. He turned the sound back up again, causing Sara to stir. 'What is it, Cal? Can't you keep that quieter?'

Cal sat agog whilst listening to the news reports.

'Concerns about the whereabouts and general welfare of a prime candidate for nomination of this position of some repute in the coming campaign, George Coney, have been played down by the City Mayor's office. Senior Security Advisor NH Steinburg issued the following statement to our outside broadcast unit.'

'We appreciate your own concerns over Mr Coney's disappearance. But I have been given to understand that Mr Coney has now purely and simply decided not to run for this position and has taken a well-earned vacation. That is all, gentlemen.'

Steinburg turned as if to leave but was called back by a barrage of questions. He kept a smile on his face but the strain could clearly be seen in his false expression.

'But what do you think has happened to make him have such a change of mind? I mean, the last time he made a public appearance, he was still talking enthusiastically about the nomination.'

'Gentlemen, I have no more information on this subject. I am sorry, but that is all I can tell you at the moment. When George Coney resurfaces I am certain he himself will have an explanation for you.'

'But you must agree, it does look highly suspicious – just disappearing like that. His wife apparently does not know his whereabouts.'

'Gentlemen, I must leave now to attend to some other matters you are all aware of: the loss of power to our systems caused by the computer virus. I would in the meantime appeal to you not to hound George if he does make an appearance. Let him make his explanation in his own good time.'

'Mr Steinburg! You say that in a way which makes me believe you do know where he is and why he has apparently given up the nomination.'

Steinburg glared at the reporter, a senior hack of many years standing. 'Mr Harris, I would appreciate it if you were not to make such assumptions. You are sailing very close to a writ from my lawyer, my friend.'

Harris made no further comment but stared back at Steinburg with his usual knowing look. Steinburg caught a glimpse of it and turned away and went back into the building.

Sara had now propped herself up as Cal had made no reply. She too noticed the photograph now being shown on the screen. 'Jeez, Cal, it's that monster who interviewed us with the mad bitch. What were they saying about him?'

Cal quickly filled her in on the story. 'Sounds like he is in a heap more trouble. Serves the bastard right... and I bet Djumbola has something to do with it. He certainly did not like that man.'

Their attention then reverted to another news report. It concerned the failure of many institutions in saving stored information attacked by the computer virus. The source had now been traced, and frantic efforts were being made to isolate the virus. The report stated that there would obviously be a period of major problems, especially with the banking system, which had been severely disrupted. All concerned were asking for the public's patience over this matter. Every effort was being made to restore systems back to normal. The pictures were of mass queues at major banks, and other disruptions elsewhere.

Cal whistled. 'Am I glad I took all my money out of these accounts now! Wonder if the rock knew what was going to eventually happen...'

'Must have done, Cal. Knew Djumbola was going to strike the way he did. Hasn't he done a good job! Very impressed. Bet there are a load of slimy individuals crying into their empty pots of gold!'

The room suddenly lit up. Cal and Sara turned to the cause of the illumination and found the two shards floating before them, becoming ever brighter as the figure loomed into view. The hood of the cloaked one slipped back revealing the stunning beauty of Sahariah.

'Greetings to the pair of you. I am come to thank you again for your efforts in assisting our line to the success achieved. Djumbola as usual has done his wonders. It was very much touch and go on this occasion, though. One slight mistake would have meant disaster, but fortunately everything went to plan. Especially after we traced the mole in our camp. Nefaurau is safely back with us. He sends his best wishes and hopes you have recovered from your injuries trying to prevent XChiang from taking him. Djumbola was the only one of us with sufficient powers to be a match for this demon. Djumbola's spell now keeps XChiang in place away from us all. But another of his kind will eventually surface. It is the way of things. Only nature is party to such secrets of why the magic requires us to be constantly battling with evil. Having said that, I do believe Djumbola has an idea too. But he will never be drawn on this, saying it is too dangerous to discuss. I will be waiting to take Djumbola back with me, as he has promised Nefaurau and myself. As you will imagine we are both so happy and relieved at this. Farewell for now.'

Sahariah waved a hand at the shards, which shone ever brighter as she took a step backwards. Then she disappeared.

'Wow! This would make some film, Sara. Who would you like to play you?' Cal was grinning like a Cheshire cat.

'I don't think anybody would be allowed to make a film this real. I mean, it would be full of so much controversy, and real people out there who are pulling the strings right now wouldn't like it. They'd get in the way of its production and that.'

'I suppose you are right, Sara. But that's a pity. We could be famous!' Cal exclaimed.

'Wouldn't want that at all, Cal. Just a nice quiet life, bringing up our family. But something tells me we are going to be needed again for more exploits.'

'That would be correct, Sara.' The shards had reignited into brilliant colours, stunning the pair as Djumbola made his entrance.

'Greetings again, Sara and Calvin! I see you have been discussing matters. I also overheard the television broadcast and Sahariah's speech to you. One of the reasons I was successful with my spell over XChiang depended on my agreeing to return with Sahariah and assist my line with the flood of evacuees expected as the rock descends on this planet. There will still be matters for you two, if you are willing to assist us from this side. A secret bridge will be devised through a portal, but I still envisage much that can still go wrong. We will have to wait and see.'

'What sort of things would you want us to do, Djumbola?' Cal asked.

'Calvin, one thing I will ask of you now is to keep this file safe. It is the one I took from George Coney's office. It has priceless information in it. I wish to devise a way to put some of it back into the system to confuse their own input. At the moment the whole system is blank, obviously. But it will only be a matter of time before they break back in. After all, I managed to break theirs, with a little luck. All they require is an equal measure and they will be in again. But I want to keep them on their toes. Especially want all the dirty money to be diverted to a special account to be used to finance our plans. Do you think you could devise this for me, Cal? I know you said your brother showed you a lot. Perhaps if I sit you down now I can open a void for you two to discuss this. That okay?'

Cal was nodding his head, at the same time feeling bewildered by the sudden amount he had just taken in. Sara watched as Djumbola relaxed Cal, muttering an incantation over him. Then he turned to Sara and whispered, 'You are most welcome to join the void and speak with your grandmother. Your choice.'

Sara thought about it for a moment and then thought, Why not? She nodded to Djumbola. Soon Sara too was in the twilight zone of dream communication. They both eventually came to, but Djumbola had disappeared again.

Sara was not as upset as she thought she might have been, considering her grandmother had admitted to having dissuaded her daughter, Sara's mother, from believing in the possibility of life after death. The air had been cleared in an adult fashion, with both of them now back to their usual natural banter.

Cal too had had a wonderful experience. Felt just like E had been in the room with him sitting side by side. They had discussed the matter Djumbola had proposed. E had given Cal a lot of pointers which he said he should write down while they were still fresh in his mind. Cal was amazed to find a notebook sitting on his lap with the information already written by him. Everything about the experience had been truly amazing.

'Wow, Sara, that was cool! Like my brother was in the room with me. He communicated all this technical info to me and asked me to write it down before I forgot it. And look, the notebook's full of the stuff he was telling me. I was actually writing it down whilst still in the dream. Fantastic!'

He handed the book to Sara, who flicked through the pages, muttering her surprise at how much it contained. 'Pretty neat and tidy for you too, Cal. But maybe it's your brother's writing through you. They call it by a special word.'

Cal took the notebook back again. Looking closer now with his glasses on, he exclaimed, 'Jeez, Sara, you're right! It is E's writing! Amazing!' He then noticed Sara staring into space, and asked, 'How did you get on, Sara? Did you patch things up?'

She just nodded, still feeling a tear close by. As much as Cal was excited and exuberant about his experience, Sara took hers a little more personally and wished to keep it to herself. 'Sorry, Cal. It's still so very new to me. Can't quite get my whole head around it all yet. It was nice and reassuring.'

Cal agreed. 'I really shouldn't be so up about it, anyway. The truth is I still haven't quite got over how he died. It was so traumatic.'

Sara sat beside Cal and put an arm around him. 'You said you would tell me about it. Would it help if you did?'

Cal thought for a moment and then slowly nodded. He described how Iain Tulley had been asked to work on a secret project closely linked with the Space Programme. Very high-tech computer knowledge was required, and E certainly fitted the bill. But something strange happened. E became very withdrawn and uncommunicative, even with Cal. He still helped Cal with his own computer education but always seemed a little distant, as though something was playing on his mind. Then one day he jumped. From the sixteenth floor. Cal had been shopping nearby, heard the commotion and went for a look. Wished he hadn't. The sight of his brother's broken body had haunted him ever since. Cal had found the note later, hidden under some computer equipment. Seemed he had been worrying about threats by people inside the space project. Them fearing E was going to spill the beans over dodgy dealings. He was being labelled a 'whistle-blower'. An accusation he absolutely hated. He couldn't take any more. In the note he apologised to Cal and all his other family and friends. There was a simple 'Goodbye chums!' at the end. It was a term he used when deleting unwanted info from the systems. Cal immediately had known what he meant by it; and just like him, with his dry sense of humour. When he had been in the mood, that is; which he certainly was not during those last few weeks of his life. So ironic, Cal thought – him making a small joke at the end of his suicide note. Deleting himself...

Cal began to sob and Sara hugged him close. 'Sorry, Cal, I shouldn't have asked you to tell me.'

Cal wiped the tears off his face. 'No, Sara. I had to get it out of me. But I don't think I will ever forgive those bastards who drove him to it. Too many like them in this world. Starts as soon as you can walk. Always someone trying to push you around. Every where you go always someone picking on you. And these fucking people always, *always*, get those jobs where they can push you around. They don't promote enough of the decent types, so there is no one really protecting our interests out there. Just got a bunch of bullies all sticking together, covering each other's backs whilst they shaft the rest of us. And this fucking term "whistle-blower": it makes me mad. Makes me want to do serious harm to those cowardly bastards. You notice when they want witnesses to come forward to assist them, it's called giving information – ratting on your friends and family, for example, because they are too thick and lazy to go and investigate the matter themselves. Even offering up rewards for such snitching. But if you find *them* doing anything wrong, the bullying streak becomes a frenzy in order to put that protective shield around themselves. All kinds of dirty tricks. And this fucking word "whistle-blower" comes out of the woodwork aimed at anyone who has the audacity to tell the truth and blow the bastards in. That's the difference, Sara. One rule for those bastards, and the rest of us can go to hell!'

'*Very well put, Calvin. Couldn't have expressed it better myself.*' The lights were back, and so too was Djumbola.

'I have been eavesdropping on the people who matter. Whatever they are putting out through the media, it is a million miles from the truth. They are in an unbelievable tangle all around the globe. The world economy is on the brink of collapse. A lot of fat rats are capsizing the ship. Without their dirty money, the strings they usually pull are becoming disconnected, leaving them hanging out to dry! I hope I do not appear to be too conceited. But I am very pleased with how things are working out. You two have no worries. I have decided to allow the shards to remain with you. They will alert us if the bogeyman comes a knocking at your door again! Obviously, with the pandemonium which is taking place out there, all thoughts on the cults of asteroid rock have been forgotten and the investigations suspended indefinitely.' Suddenly Djumbola began to sway. He looked about to fall.

The pair were on their feet rushing to his aid but he waved them to be still. 'It is alright. Thank you for your concern. I have taken more out of myself than I had realised. I just wished to update you both before I leave for home. *Home*... strange for me to be saying that after so long!'

Djumbola held his hands out to the shards, which flew over to him. Taking one in each hand, he gripped them, causing them to glow brighter. Then he released them. They flew back over to the pair, one landing on Cal's shoulder and the other in Sara's lap. They were emitting new found warmth and serenity.

'Sahariah will be waiting to take me back now. And I am ready. I must admit to being a little homesick. I never thought I would ever feel that way again. Not since a child have I felt this so strongly. Nefaurau is back safely with his mother now. Nature's magic allowed my request because it is written in its book. Nothing comes between mother and son. Nature's balance relies on it.'

Tears were now in Sara's eyes. Cal too was gulping them back. Djumbola moved forward and hugged Cal. 'Good fortune, Calvin. Look after yourself and this wonderful lady of yours.'

Then, turning to Sara, he took her hand and placed a shining cross in it. 'For your child. My gift. I have been so very pleased to know both of you. Live happily. That is my wish.'

Sara started to throw her arms around him but he had disappeared. Tears were now streaming down her face. '*Men*! Damn them!'

Postscript

For all the downtrodden, misplaced, displaced, disaffected, disabused ever wandering, ever wondering: this story is dedicated to you. Never give up hope. For nature's eye sees everything. Always watching. Remembering all. It will have the last word.
   Djumbola Arun Altu

Printed in the United Kingdom
by Lightning Source UK Ltd.
104246UKS00001B/3